I0605746

MOTORSPORTS ENCYCLOPEDIAS

THE NASCAR ENCYCLOPEDIA

BY PRIYANKA LAMICHHANE

Encyclopedias

An Imprint of Abdo Reference
abdobooks.com

TABLE OF CONTENTS

SPRINT
RACE
D/M.HENRIQUES
MA7S
COFFEE TO GO
ACTION 360°
11

HISTORY OF NASCAR

The history of NASCAR is a story of speed, competition, and American tradition, and it all began with a man named Bill France Sr.

France developed a passion for racing as a teenager after watching local races around his hometown of Washington, DC. After getting married, he opened a car service station, but in 1935, he and his family decided to move to Daytona Beach, Florida, for warmer weather. Car racing was already popular there. France

Bill France Sr.

Stock car race in Daytona Beach, Feb. 14, 1953

FUN FACT

The first NASCAR National Headquarters was Bill France's house in Daytona Beach. The house is still there today.

decided to get involved in organizing races.

France noticed there were a lot of problems in the racing world. Drivers were not getting paid the money they were promised, there weren't enough race rules, and the races weren't properly promoted. Not enough people knew about them. In 1948, France founded NASCAR, an organization to create race rules, to protect and pay drivers, and to promote the races.

NASCAR IN THE KNOW

The beginning of car racing in the United States dates back to the Prohibition era of the 1920s. During that time, alcohol could not be made, sold, or transported. But some people illegally made and sold it anyway. To transport their alcohol, they modified their cars to be faster and drive better. Drivers soon started competing to see whose cars were fastest. The sport of car racing in the United States was born!

NASCAR'S FIRST RACE

In 1948, the first NASCAR race took place in Daytona Beach. More than 14,000 people came to watch. Less than a year later, the organization grew to host 52 races. By 1949, NASCAR held the first Strictly Stock race for new model cars at the old Charlotte Fairgrounds Speedway in North

Spectators watch a race at Daytona Beach in 1955.

1953 NASCAR race car

Carolina. This race would later become known as the NASCAR Cup Series.

Eventually, France began to build special raceways just for NASCAR. The Daytona International Speedway opened in 1958. It was 2.5 miles (4 km) around. That same year, the first Daytona 500 race was held. Today, the Daytona 500 is still one of the most popular NASCAR races.

FUN FACT

Tickets to the first NASCAR race were only $2.50.

NASCAR IN THE KNOW

NASCAR stands for the National Association for Stock Car Auto Racing. When NASCAR began, the race cars were the same as those that could be driven on the streets. Soon, these regular "stock" cars were modified to make them faster. Today, NASCAR cars are built specifically for racing. They need to be fast, easy to maneuver, and built with extra safety features to protect drivers.

NASCAR MAKES ITS TELEVISION DEBUT

After more than two decades of entertaining fans at the tracks, NASCAR made its live television debut in 1979. Before this time, only short clips of races were broadcast on television and only once a week. But on February 18, 1979, CBS aired the complete Daytona 500 for the first time.

The live television broadcast of the 1979 Daytona 500 helped increase NASCAR's popularity.

A huge winter blizzard on the East Coast kept a large portion of the US population at home. This meant there would be many people watching. But there was a major problem at the racetrack. Heavy rains had left the track soaked. Back then, there wasn't a way to dry the track quickly like there is today. France decided to go on with the race, but it would happen under their "caution" status. This meant drivers had to drive more carefully and more slowly than usual.

Famous NASCAR driver Richard Petty was the winner of the 1979 Daytona 500, the first to be aired on television.

CBS aired the three-and-a-half hour Daytona 500 across the country. After a few laps around the track, it dried out enough for the caution rules to be dropped. More than 15 million people watched the live race, helping to make NASCAR popular across the country.

TIMELINE

1948
Bill France Sr. created the National Association for Stock Car Auto Racing in Daytona Beach, Florida.

JUNE 19, 1949
NASCAR held the Strictly Stock race. This later became the NASCAR Cup Series. Sara Christian was the first woman to race in this series. She came in 14th place.

FEBRUARY 20, 1977
Janet Guthrie became the first woman to race in the Daytona 500, finishing in 12th place.

1940s | 1950s | 1960s | 1970s

FEBRUARY 15, 1948
NASCAR held it first race at Daytona Beach. The winning car was a Ford driven by Red Byron.

FEBRUARY 22, 1959
The first Daytona 500 took place at the new Daytona International Speedway.

DECEMBER 1, 1963
Wendell Scott became the first Black driver to win a race in NASCAR's main series.

1979
NASCAR was broadcast live on television for the first time.

MAY 2010
NASCAR held its first Hall of Fame ceremony. NASCAR founder Bill France Sr. and superstar Richard Petty were two of five people inducted.

FEBRUARY 2022
NASCAR's "Next Gen" car model with the latest technology was introduced.

1980s | 1990s | 2000s | 2010s | 2020s

NOVEMBER 15, 1992
Jeff Gordon raced for the first time. He would become one of NASCAR's most famous drivers.

JANUARY 2003
The NASCAR Research and Development Center opened in North Carolina as a place to test car safety.

DIAGRAM OF A NASCAR RACE CAR

There are many parts to a NASCAR race car, and each has a purpose. Some help keep the car safe; others help the car go fast.

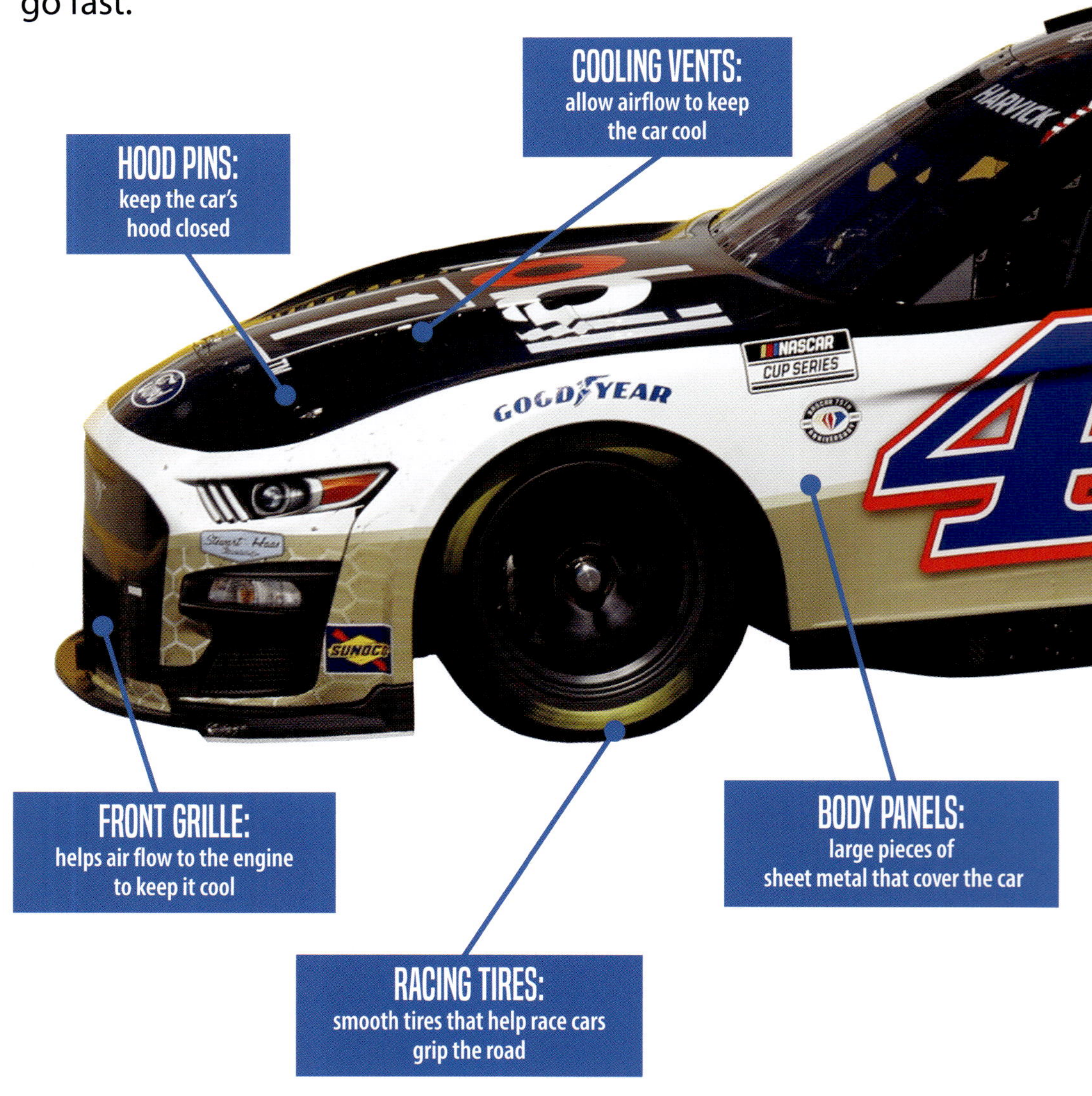

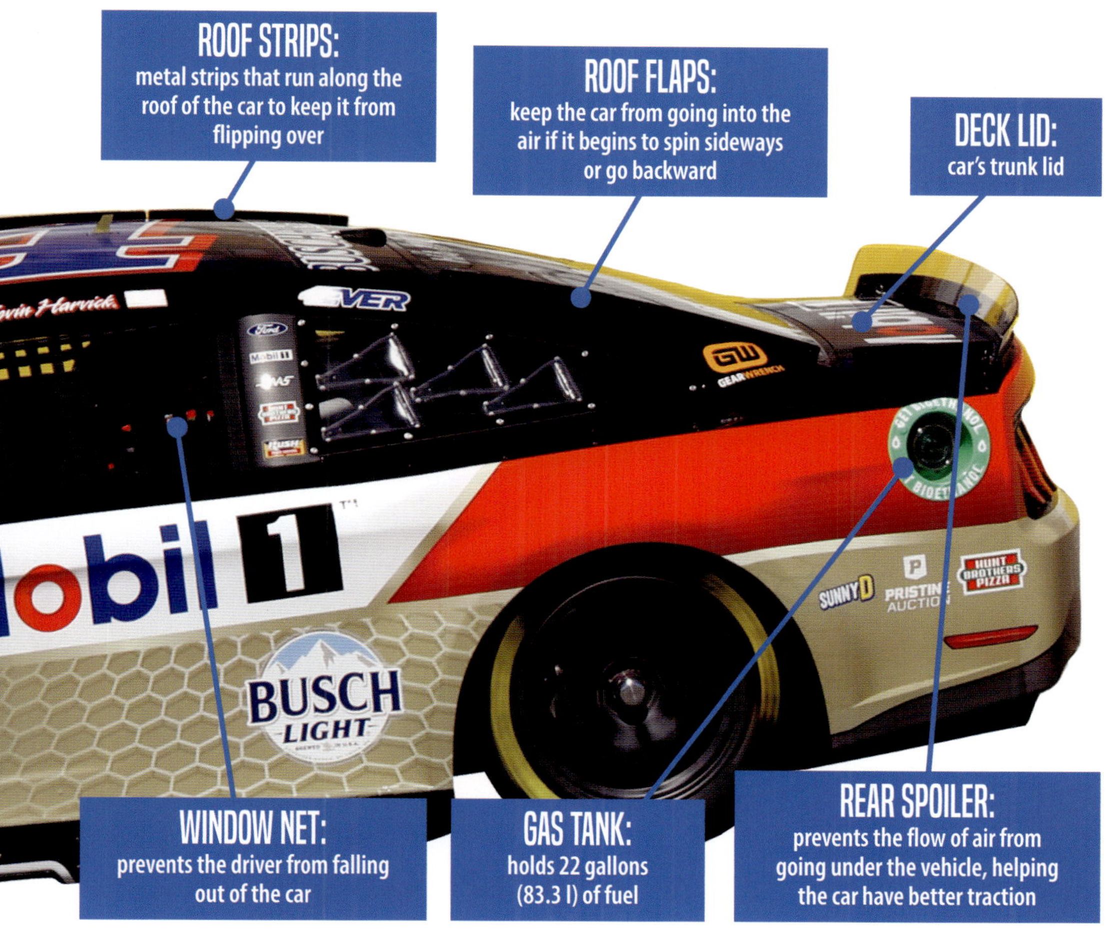

NASCAR IN THE KNOW

NASCAR race cars are built with a strong frame made from steel tubes. The roll cage is the thickest part of the frame. It protects the driver if the car rolls over or crashes. The frame also includes tubes that are the first to crush in a crash, allowing the engine to drop out from the bottom of the car. The engine can catch fire in a crash, so it's important to get it away from the driver quickly.

BUILDING A NASCAR RACE CAR

NASCAR builds only two types of cars: short track cars and superspeedway cars. Short track cars are built for tracks that are less than 1 mile (1.6 km) around. On these tracks, cars have to make very tight turns and drive a bit slower. A larger grille on the front allows a lot of airflow to cool the engine. Superspeedway cars are built for longer, straighter tracks where

short track car

superspeedway car

Power is generated in an engine's cylinders.

turns are not as tight. The cars go fast enough that they get a lot of airflow, so their grilles are smaller.

All teams have to follow the same rules when building their cars. Engines and cars have to be the same size. These rules ensure no team has an unfair advantage over the others.

- **Engines:** Engines must have V-8 power. V-8 engines have eight cylinders that are in two rows of four.
- **Horsepower:** NASCAR race cars are allowed to go up to a maximum of 670 horsepower during a race.
- **Size:** In the Cup Series, cars must be 193.4 inches (491 cm) long and 78.6 inches (200 cm) wide. In the Xfinity Series, cars are 203.8 inches (518 cm) long and 75 inches (191 cm) wide. NASCAR trucks are 206.5 inches (525 cm) long and 80 inches (203 cm) wide.

FUN FACT

It takes 10 days to install the body of just one race car!

SPECIAL FEATURES OF A NASCAR RACE CAR

NASCAR race cars have some special features that make them different from the cars most people drive. Modifications to the cars make them more durable, easier to maneuver, and faster.

SMOOTH TIRES

Instead of being filled with air, NASCAR tires are filled with nitrogen. Too much moisture in a hot and fast-moving tire makes it harder to control the car. Nitrogen has less moisture than air. On the outside, NASCAR tires are completely smooth. Regular car tires have tread, which removes mud, water, or snow and helps the tires grip the road.

TANK OF STEEL

In these race cars, a fuel tank, known as a fuel cell, is built with safety as a top priority. The fuel cells have a layer of steel on

The tires' smooth surface allows the cars to have full contact with the track for a better grip.

Since 1997, Goodyear has been the exclusive tire supplier of NASCAR.

the outside and a layer of hard plastic on the inside. They are also filled with foam. The foam keeps gasoline from splashing around and from exploding by keeping most air out of the cell. If an explosion happens, the foam is able to absorb it.

FUN FACT

There are currently three car makers that build cars for NASCAR: Chevrolet, Ford, and Toyota.

POWERFUL PLASTIC

The windshield of a NASCAR race car isn't made of glass. It is made of a special plastic called Lexan. Lexan is lighter than glass, which makes the car lighter too. Lexan is also difficult to break. Airplane windows are made of a similar plastic.

NASCAR RACE SERIES

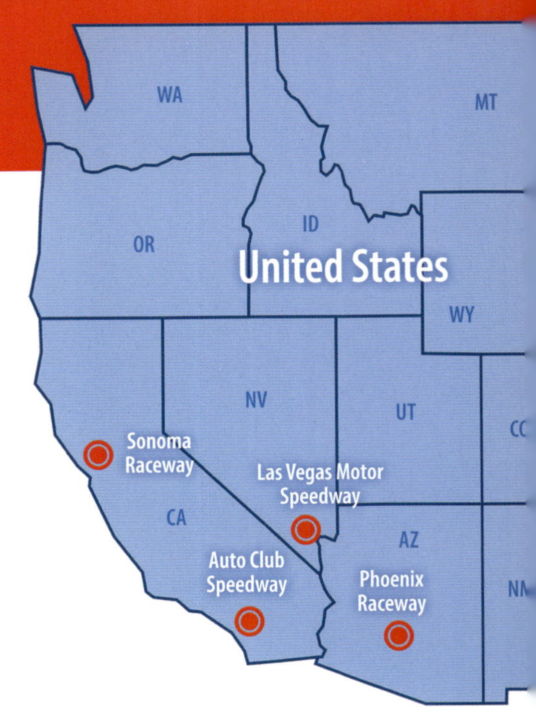

Crowds attend NASCAR races all over the United States and in a few places internationally. In the United States, there are three race series: the Cup Series, which is the highest level of racing; the Xfinity Series, the second tier of NASCAR racing; and the Truck Series, the third level of racing. Drivers in the Xfinity Series often move up to the Cup Series. Drivers in the Truck Series are often driving at the national level for the first time. The NASCAR series races take place at numerous raceways across the country.

NASCAR race cars are owned by various organizations that build teams of drivers, cars, and people to take care of the vehicles. Each team is made up of four cars, all made by the same car maker. A team shares resources such as mechanics and engineers. When it's time to race, however, each car

A crew chief manages everything that happens in the pit.

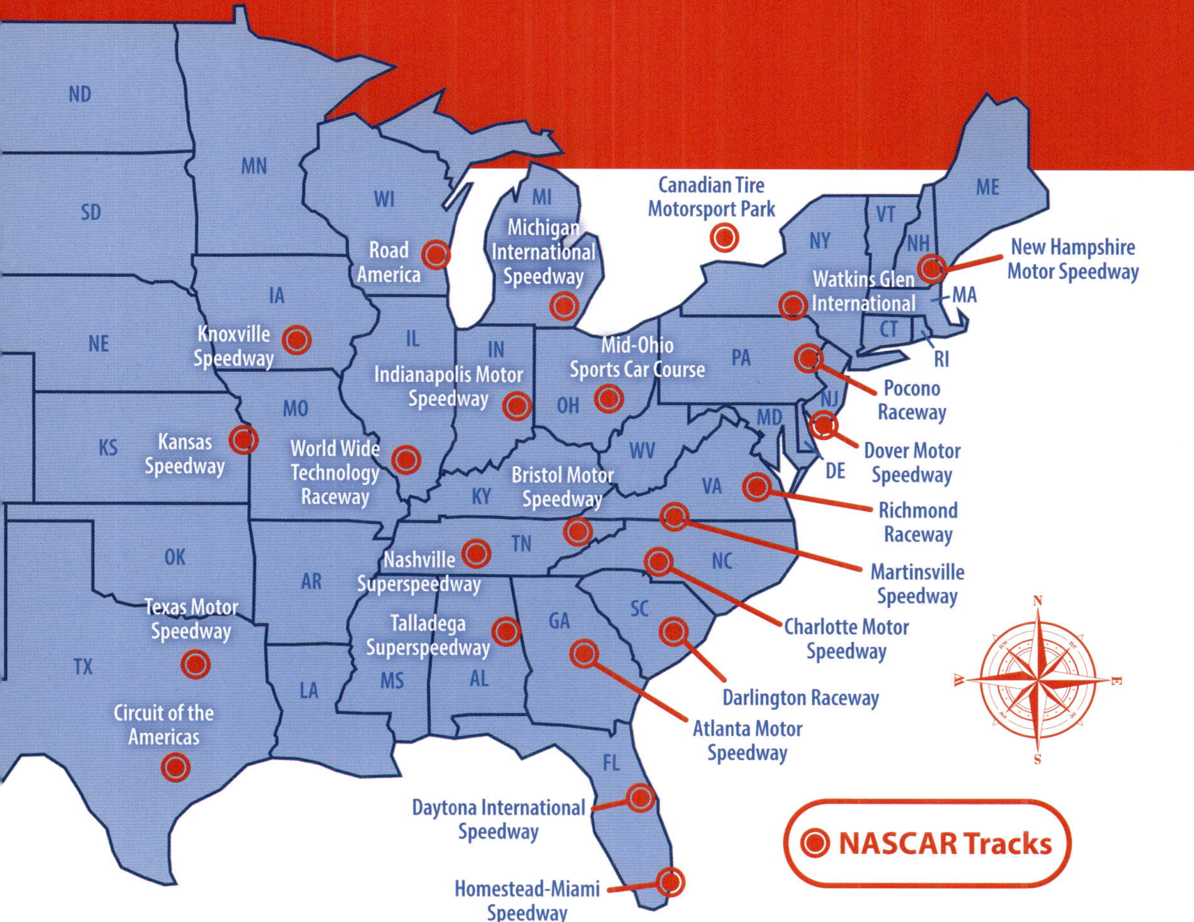

races for itself, not for its team. Each NASCAR team is made up of about 100 people. This includes the pit crew, the team owner, the team manager, the road crew, and many others.

BY THE NUMBERS

Number of Cup Series races: 36
Number of Xfinity Series races: 33
Number of Truck Series races: 23
Driver with the most NASCAR wins: Richard Petty, 200 wins
Team with the most wins: Hendrick Motorsports, 14 Cup Series championships

Trucks that race in the NASCAR Truck Series run on smaller tires than regular trucks.

NASCAR CRAFTSMAN TRUCK SERIES

The NASCAR Craftsman Truck Series is named after its sponsor, Craftsman Tools. The series is a set of 23 races that race pickup trucks instead of cars. The trucks have been modified for racing. It is where newer, younger race car drivers train and practice. Some of the best NASCAR drivers started here. The races are held on many of the same speedways where other NASCAR races take place.

In 1991, a few truck racers came up with the idea for the NASCAR Truck Series. They spent several years figuring out how to build trucks that could race on the speedways, and they promoted the idea with NASCAR fans. Finally in 1995, the first NASCAR Truck Series race was held.

NASCAR IN THE KNOW

The ARCA Menards Series is a minor league car racing series. ARCA stands for Auto Racing Club of America. Many of the ARCA drivers will go on to drive in the Truck Series and continue to make their way to NASCAR's two top series. Usually, ARCA drivers will race as a pre-show before a NASCAR race. They use older NASCAR Cup and Xfinity Series cars.

ARCA Series car

NASCAR CUP SERIES

The NASCAR Cup Series has 17 teams and 36 races. The races take place at all the NASCAR raceways across the country. The race is divided into two segments. The first segment is made of 26 races. The top 16 drivers move on to the second segment of 10 races. This is known as the NASCAR playoffs. Four drivers are eliminated in four rounds of racing. The final stage of the race takes place when only four drivers are left. The winner of this round is the series champion.

Martinsville Speedway, Ridgeway, Virginia

NASCAR IN THE KNOW

A NASCAR race can be anywhere between 150 and 600 laps. On average, a race is 400 miles (644 km) long and takes about three hours. The shortest NASCAR lap in a Cup Series is 0.53 miles (0.9 km) long at the Martinsville Speedway in Virginia. The longest lap is 3.4 miles (5.5 km) at the Circuit of the Americas in Austin, Texas.

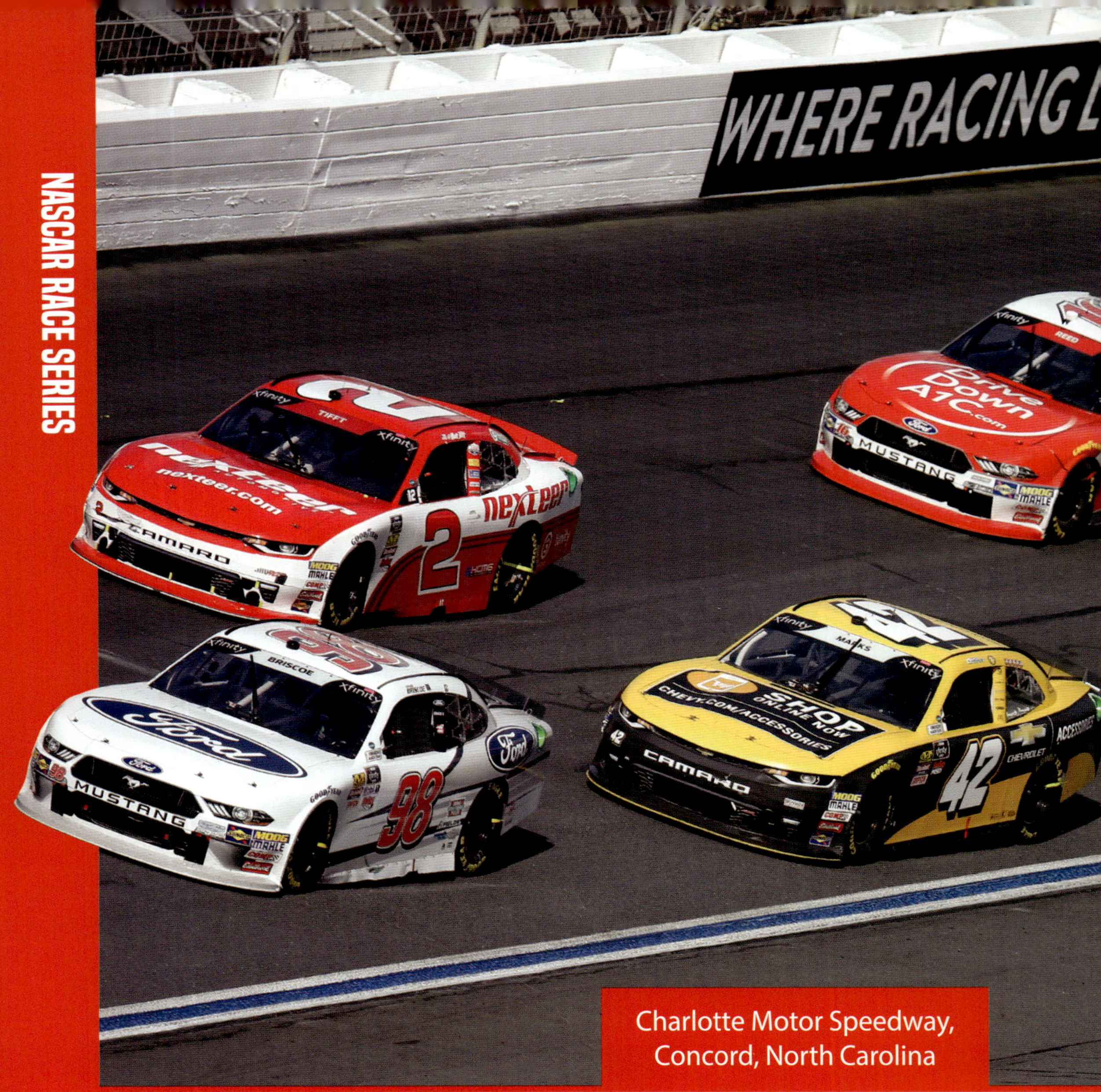

Charlotte Motor Speedway, Concord, North Carolina

NASCAR XFINITY SERIES

The Xfinity Series started in the 1950s. It was called the Sportsman Division. By 1968, it was renamed the Late Model Sportsman Series. It changed names a few more times over the years. In 2014, it became the Xfinity Series.

There are 36 drivers in each Xfinity race. Many of them are working to make it to the Cup Series. Xfinity races are usually held a day before Cup Series races. The races are held all over the United States. This series has also taken place in other countries including Mexico and Canada. In 2005, the first international Xfinity Series race was held in Mexico City, Mexico.

FUN FACT

From 1956 to 1959, NASCAR held races for convertibles, which were popular at the time.

Cole Custer celebrates after winning the 2023 NASCAR Xfinity Series Championship.

NASCAR AROUND THE WORLD

Over the past 75 years, NASCAR has come a long way from its origins in Daytona Beach, Florida. The organization holds numerous races every year and has speedways all over the United States. NASCAR has now become international. The organization holds races in more than 10 countries. It has regular series in three other countries and a single series that is held in a number of countries in Europe.

BRAZIL

BRASIL SPRINT RACE

The Brasil Sprint Race has been going on for more than 10 years. But in 2023, the series joined NASCAR, becoming the

Autódromo Internacional Ayrton Senna in Brazil

Pedro Rodriguez

organization's newest racing series. It is also NASCAR's first series in South America. The Brasil Sprint Race is made up of eight races, held at five different tracks around the country.

MEXICO

NASCAR MEXICO SERIES

Many Mexican drivers have raced for NASCAR. The first was Pedro Rodriguez, who raced in the NASCAR Cup Series from 1959 to 1971. Over the years, NASCAR built a relationship with Mexico's racing community, and in 2006, the first Mexico Series event was held. It has been running ever since. It is Mexico's top tier of stock car racing and was NASCAR's first international racing competition held outside of the United States.

Pinty's Series cars race at the Autodrome Chaudiere in Quebec, Canada.

CANADA

NASCAR PINTY'S SERIES

NASCAR Pinty's Series is the top stock car racing series in Canada. Races take place from May to September, when the Canadian weather is warm enough to race. Drivers travel to five different provinces, racing all across the country. Fans can watch races in person and on television. Race commentators speak in both French and English, Canada's two official languages.

Pinty's Series trophy

EUROPE

NASCAR WHELEN EURO SERIES

The NASCAR Whelen EURO Series started out as its own event, known as the Racecar Series. It began in 2008 with races in France. It soon gained many fans. By 2010, the racing series became international and was renamed the Euro Racecar Series. In 2011, races took place in Germany, the Netherlands, and Great Britain. One year later, the Euro Racecar Series became part of NASCAR. It was renamed the Euro Racecar NASCAR Touring Series and eventually the NASCAR Whelen EURO Series.

FUN FACT

NASCAR races are shown on television in 195 countries and territories around the world.

Cars compete at a NASCAR Whelen Euro Series race in Valencia, Spain.

THE RACE CARS

NASCAR race cars have come a long way since 1948. They not only look different on the outside, but they also are different on the inside. There have been seven generations of cars, and from one version to the next, making cars safer has been the top priority.

GENERATION 1 (1948 TO 1966)

The cars used in NASCAR early races were regular street cars. There were no special changes made to them. The winner of NASCAR's first race in 1949 was Jim Roper. He raced a borrowed car that he drove from his home in Kansas to the race at the Charlotte Speedway in North Carolina.

The Hudson Hornet was the inspiration for the character Doc Hudson in the movie *Cars*.

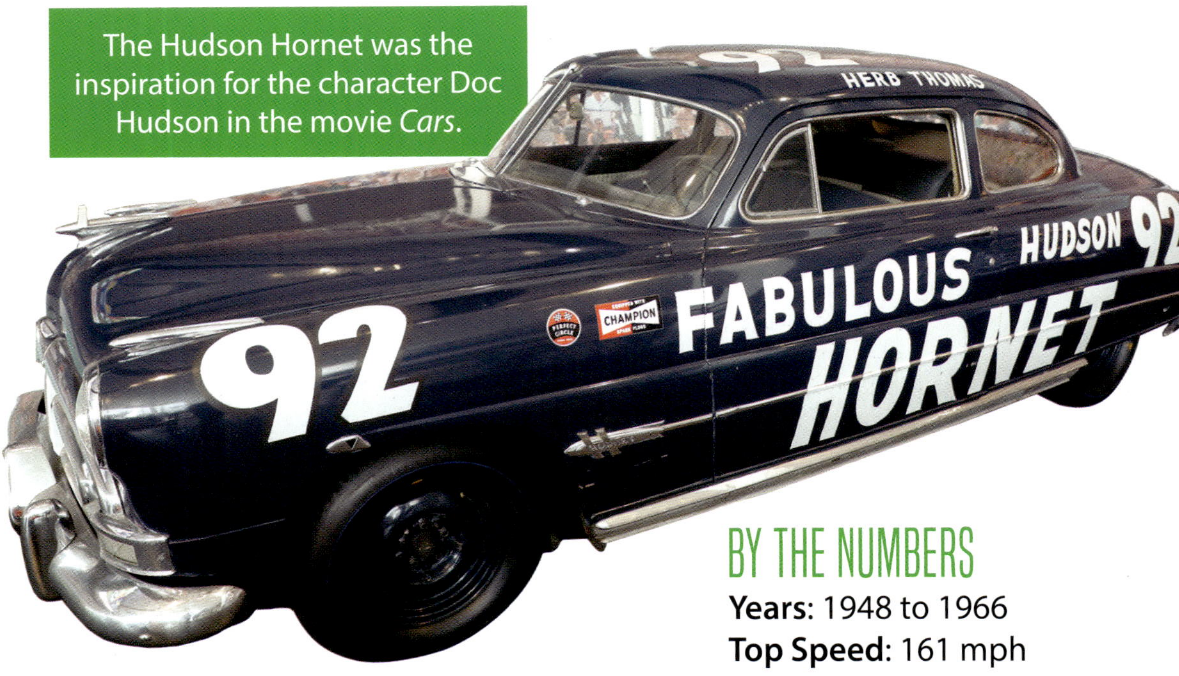

BY THE NUMBERS

Years: 1948 to 1966
Top Speed: 161 mph (259 kmh)

Without a door to open, all drivers were required to enter and exit through the windows.

GENERATION 2 (1967 TO 1980)

Frames and roll cages were added to Generation 2 cars. Car doors were also welded shut to prevent them from flying open. Eventually, cars were built without any doors at all, making the structure stronger and safer.

BY THE NUMBERS

Years: 1967 to 1980
Top Speed: 190 mph (305.8 kmh)

GENERATION 3 (1981 TO 1991)

Generation 3 cars had shorter wheelbases and bigger spoilers.

BY THE NUMBERS

Years: 1981 to 1991
Top Speed: 213 mph (343 kmh)

A shorter wheelbase allows a car to turn faster and more easily.

GENERATION 4 (1992 TO 2007)

When Generation 4 cars came around, they looked similar to cars from previous generations. But Generation 4 cars were built with fiberglass instead of steel, which made them lighter.

BY THE NUMBERS

Years: 1992 to 2006
Top Speed: 200 mph (322 kmh)

The bodies of Generation 4 cars were stretched and bent to maximize aerodynamics.

The Generation 5 car was so improved that it earned the nickname "Car of Tomorrow."

GENERATION 5 (2007 TO 2012)

The Generation 5 cars made big leaps when it came to safety. The bodies were built to be more symmetrical than the Generation 4 cars. This helped reduce the effects of aerodynamics to allow the car's build and driver's skill to play a bigger role in performance. A front splitter was added to the underside of the front bumper. The splitter made the cars faster while also making them more stable at high speeds. These cars also had rear wings in the back that helped move air up, which pushed the car down.

NASCAR IN THE KNOW

A window net on the driver's side window helps air flow and allows a quick exit for the driver. The passenger side has a window, but it is made with plastic, not glass.

BY THE NUMBERS

Years: 2007 to 2012
Top Speed: 190 mph (306 kmh)

GENERATION 6 (2013 TO 2021)

NASCAR worked very closely with car brands Toyota, Ford, and Chevrolet on the development of Generation 6 cars. One of the goals was to make them look more like the cars seen on the road. This would help increase sales. The second goal was to continue to improve the safety of the race cars. Though the cars were bulkier than those of the previous generations, they were faster and tougher.

BY THE NUMBERS

Years: 2013 to 2021
Top Speed: 200 mph (321.9 kmh)

FUN FACT

The Next Gen cars were supposed to debut in 2021, but they were delayed due to the COVID-19 global pandemic.

Kyle Busch races in a Toyota, 2019.

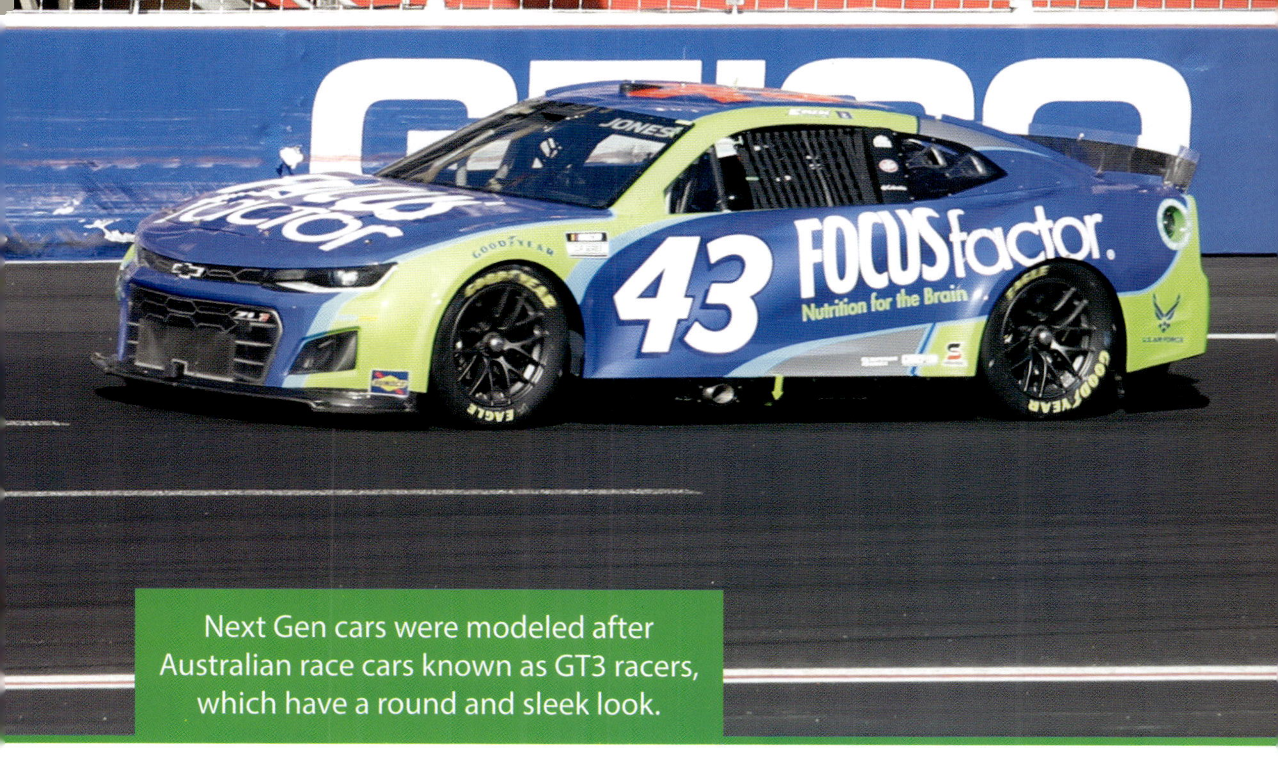

Next Gen cars were modeled after Australian race cars known as GT3 racers, which have a round and sleek look.

NEXT GEN (2022 TO PRESENT)

NASCAR's Next Gen race cars made their debut in 2022 looking sleeker and more modern than any of the previous models. There were upgrades made to the safety and technological features, and the latest technology was used to build the cars. There were also changes made to the wheels. They got bigger: from 15 inches (38 cm) wide to 18 inches (46 cm) wide. Wider wheels are easier to replace during pit stops.

BY THE NUMBERS

Years: 2022 to present
Top Speed: 191 mph (307.4 kmh)

NASCAR IN THE KNOW

The headlights on a NASCAR race car are actually stickers placed to make the cars look more like the street cars we see on the road. NASCAR doesn't race at night, so headlights aren't needed.

EVOLUTION OF NASCAR CUP RACE CARS

NASCAR Cup Series race cars have come a long way over more than 70 years.

GENERATION 1 (1948 TO 1966)

1965 Ford Galaxie

- Seat belts were required.
- Cars had doors; they were eventually bolted shut.
- No modifications were allowed.

GENERATION 2 (1967 TO 1980)

1977 Dodge Charger

- Teams could make some adjustments to the chassis but not the frame.
- New safety features were added to handle the new superspeedways.
- NASCAR partnered with manufacturers to build cars.
- Cars still had doors, but they didn't open.

GENERATION 3 (1981 TO 1991)

- Cars had no doors at all.
- Spoilers were added.
- Car bodies were streamlined.

1991 Chevy Lumina

2006 Ford Fusion

GENERATION 4 (1992 TO 2006)

- Fiberglass replaced steel car bodies.
- New aerodynamics were improved.
- Cars looked less like showroom counterparts.

2012 Chevy Impala

GENERATION 5 (2007 TO 2012)

- With more advanced technology, major safety upgrades were made.
- A larger rear wing was added.

2013 Ford Fusion

GENERATION 6 (2013 TO 2021)

- Car models were bulkier and faster.
- Cars featured advanced aerodynamics and a larger rear wing.

NEXT GEN (2022 TO PRESENT)

- Car bodies were sleeker and more rounded.
- Manufacturers had more freedom to shape the cars to look more like their own brand.

2022 Toyota Camry

NASCAR CUP SERIES CARS

FORD MUSTANG GT

NASCAR's Ford Mustang GT was built for speed with a powerful V-8 engine. The newest Mustangs also have a special roof that allows drivers to get in and out without having to remove their helmets. The inside of the car resembles the cockpit of an airplane. It took two years to develop the car. It is 51 inches (130 cm) tall with a 110-inch (279-cm) wheelbase.

CHEVROLET CAMARO ZL1

The Chevy Camaro ZL1 has been one of Chevrolet's best-performing street cars. It was used in the Xfinity Series for a few years before moving into the Cup Series. The car was also tested by multiple drivers before its entry into NASCAR's top racing series.

2021 Chevrolet Camaro ZL1

The wheels on the Toyota Camry TRD are partially made of aluminum to make them as light as possible.

TOYOTA CAMRY TRD

Like the Ford Mustang GT, the Toyota Camry TRD was built to allow the car to be converted from gas to hybrid or electric power in the future. The car has bigger wheels along with larger brakes to make sure the car stops properly. It features changes that are firsts for a NASCAR car: a deeper front splitter and a huge diffuser in the back. A diffuser is shaped to allow for better aerodynamics.

FUN FACT

The minimum weight limit on all NASCAR cars is 3,400 pounds (1,542 kg). This includes the weight of the driver and a full tank of gas.

The Ford Mustang GT can reach speeds of up to 180 miles per hour (290 kmh).

NASCAR XFINITY SERIES CARS

FORD MUSTANG GT

There are many similarities among the Cup Series and Xfinity Series Mustangs, but the Xfinity Series cars have a shorter wheelbase. These smaller cars can hold more fuel in their tanks than the Cup Series cars, but they don't race as many laps.

This car can reach speeds of up to 180 miles per hour (290 kmh). NASCAR began using modified Ford Mustangs full-time in the Xfinity Series in 2011. In 2020, Ford unveiled a brand-new, modern car model that debuted at the 2020 Daytona 500.

CHEVROLET CAMARO SS

Chevy has been a NASCAR regular for more than 50 years. In 2001, the Camaro SS was the winning vehicle in 15 of the 33 races it competed in.

A Camaro SS at a pit stop

The body of the NASCAR Camaro SS looks very similar to the street model, but under the hood, the two cars are totally different. The racing version has a larger, more powerful engine.

TOYOTA SUPRA

The Toyota Supra made its NASCAR debut in 2019 at the Daytona 500. Before racing in NASCAR, the Supra was used as a race car in Japan.

The first model of the car, called a prototype, was red, white, and black.

The Supra has a powerful V-8 engine and spoilers on the back.

NASCAR TRUCK SERIES TRUCKS

Trucks are what make the NASCAR Truck Series a unique event. NASCAR trucks race on shorter speedways. Trucks don't move the same way the smaller race cars do, and the truck races do not last as long as Cup and Xfinity races.

FORD F-150

The Ford F-150 was redesigned for the 2022 season. It is not like the F-150s on the street. This version is low to the ground, like all models in the series, and is made of materials that make it lighter than the regular

FUN FACT

NASCAR truck beds are closed. An open bed would get in the way of airflow, and things could fall into it!

The Ford F-150 has been used in NASCAR Truck Series races since 1994.

All NASCAR vehicles are built with steel frames and have many fire safety measures.

trucks. This helps it move faster on the track. The latest Ford F-150 debuted at the Daytona International Speedway in February 2022.

CHEVROLET SILVERADO

The latest NASCAR Silverado has a new bumper and grille to make it look a bit more like the showroom model. But the racing version of the Chevrolet Silverado still looks quite different from the Silverado trucks on the road. This truck holds the record for the winningest truck in the Truck Series.

TOYOTA TUNDRA 8.51

The first Toyota Tundra joined NASCAR in 2004. The latest Tundra model debuted in 2022 with a new body frame. The Toyota Tundra has had a strong racing record for two decades.

EVOLUTION OF NASCAR TRUCKS

The first NASCAR Truck Series was held in 1995. But the idea for the Truck Series took some convincing. NASCAR officials were not sure racing trucks would be a fan-pleaser, and they turned down the idea at first. Then the idea was brought directly to owners Bill and Jim France a few months later, and they were convinced to give it a try. Four races were held in 1994 as a preview for what was to come in the official debut season in 1995.

2010 Toyota

NASCAR trucks race in 2019.

The first official race of the Truck Series took place on February 5, 1995. There were 33 trucks in total: 3 Dodges, 17 Chevrolets, and 13 Fords. Since then, Toyota trucks have been added to the mix, and over the years, the trucks have evolved into the modern vehicles they are today.

2023 Toyota

THE RACETRACKS

All NASCAR tracks started as dirt raceways, but NASCAR officials and drivers soon noticed that dirt tracks did not allow cars to perform at their best. Soon, NASCAR started paving racetracks. Today, NASCAR races take place on numerous tracks around the country. Some are still dirt.

There are four main types of tracks: short tracks, intermediate tracks, superspeedways, and road courses. Most tracks are ovals or irregular ovals. Short tracks are usually less than a mile. Intermediate tracks are about 1.5 miles (2.4 km) long. Superspeedways are the longest. One lap on a

Superspeedways have steep sides, called banks, which help to keep fast cars on the track as they race around curves.

The area inside the middle of the track is known as the infield.

superspeedway is more than 2 miles (3.2 km). Road courses are longer tracks that run on regular streets or tracks meant to be like streets. They are not oval-shaped. Instead, they have winding turns.

BY THE NUMBERS

Laps in a NASCAR race: 150 to 600
Total number of NASCAR tracks: 42
Longest track: 2.66 miles (4.3 km), Talladega Superspeedway
Shortest track: 0.25 miles (0.4 km), Los Angeles Memorial Coliseum

Each track has an area for pit stops called pit road. When a car needs to be serviced, it pulls off onto the pit road. Tracks are also surrounded by grandstands. That's where the spectators and fans sit.

ATLANTA MOTOR SPEEDWAY

The Atlanta Motor Speedway has hosted NASCAR races since it opened in 1960. It is known to have a rough track surface, which can wear down tires and slow down driving. But NASCAR drivers say it makes driving more fun.

Atlanta Motor Speedway

FUN FACT

Alternative tracks are used for other car and motorcycle racing events.

TRACK STATS

- **Shape**: Quad-oval
- **Seating**: 71,000
- **Length**: 1.54 miles (2.5 km)
- **Location**: Hampton, Georgia

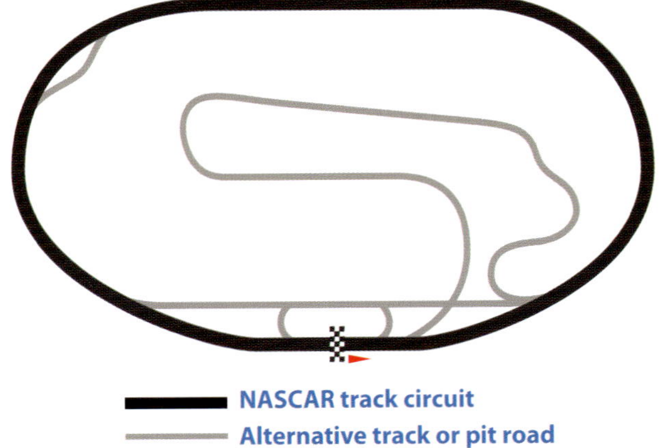

The Auto Club Speedway in California hosted both IndyCar and stock car races.

AUTO CLUB SPEEDWAY

The Auto Club Speedway, known for its wide, 2-mile (3.2-km) raceway, has been a favorite among NASCAR drivers and fans. But it is being demolished. It will be replaced with a high-banked oval track that will be a half mile (0.8 km) around.

TRACK STATS

- **Shape**: D-shaped oval
- **Seating**: 122,000, (2023)
- **Length**: 2 miles (3.2 km), (2023)
- **Location**: Fontana, California

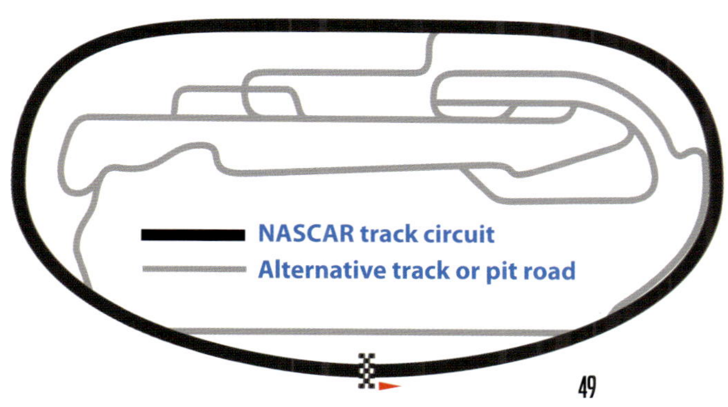

FUN FACT

Small pieces of rubber and asphalt that collect on top of the track are known as marbles.

"Racing the Way It Oughta Be" is a song about watching a NASCAR race at Bristol Motor Speedway.

BRISTOL MOTOR SPEEDWAY

Bristol Motor Speedway is known as "The Last Great Colosseum" because it looks a little like the ancient Colosseum in Rome, Italy. The track has high turns, and the grandstands are high over the track, which makes it feel like an amphitheater.

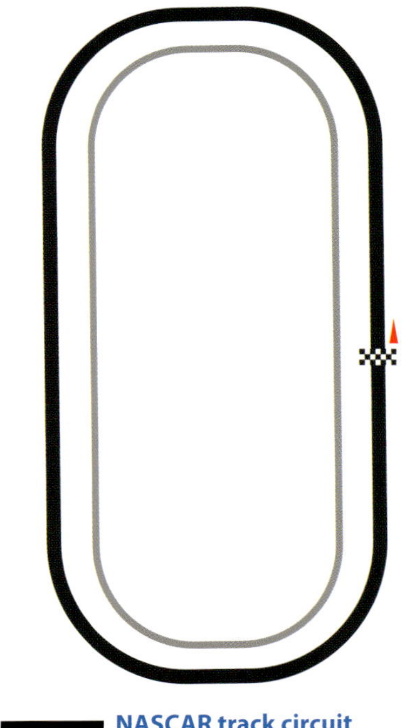

TRACK STATS

- **Shape**: Oval (concrete and dirt track)
- **Seating**: 153,000
- **Length**: 0.533 miles (0.86 km)
- **Location**: Bristol, Tennessee

CHARLOTTE MOTOR SPEEDWAY

Charlotte Motor Speedway is a special place. It has a rich NASCAR history and is home to the Coca-Cola 600, one of NASCAR's most highly regarded races. It is also close to the NASCAR Hall of Fame, which is located in downtown Charlotte, North Carolina.

TRACK STATS

- **Shape**: Quad-oval
- **Seating**: 89,000
- **Length**: 1.5 miles (2.4 km)
- **Location**: Concord, North Carolina

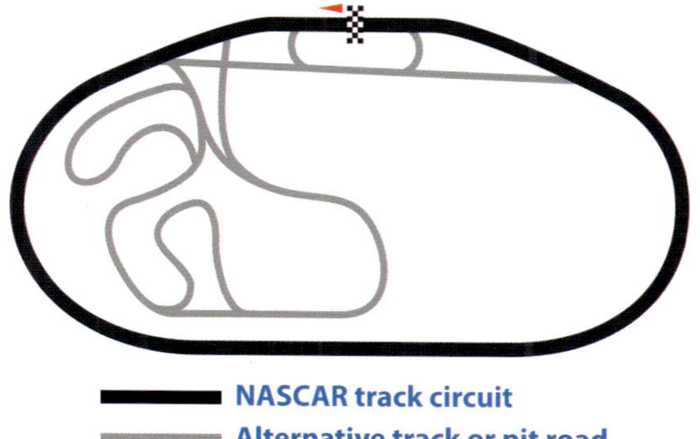

Some pit stops are located in the infield.

Chicagoland Speedway is the largest sporting facility in the state of Illinois.

CHICAGOLAND SPEEDWAY

Chicagoland Speedway was a place to see NASCAR's exciting action for more than 20 years. The Speedway held its first race in 2001. It hosted the NASCAR Cup Series from 2001 to 2019. But NASCAR has not raced at the track since 2019. The 2020 Cup Series at Chicagoland was canceled due to the COVID-19 pandemic, and the Series never returned to the track. The Chicagoland Speedway is now being used for other racing activities such as the SuperMotocross Playoffs.

FUN FACT

NASCAR races will stop if the tracks get wet.

TRACK STATS

- **Shape**: Oval
- **Seating**: 47,000
- **Length**: 1.5 miles (2.4 km)
- **Location**: Joliet, Illinois

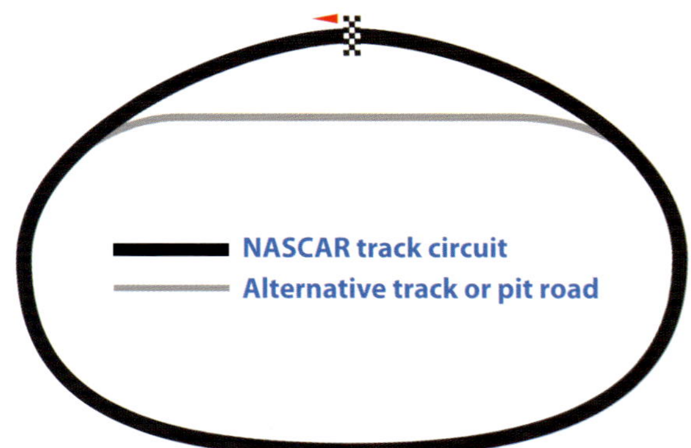

CIRCUIT OF THE AMERICAS

Circuit of The Americas is known for its dramatic elevation change of 130 feet (40 m), providing a fun and challenging racing experience for NASCAR drivers. It hosts NASCAR's Texas Grand Prix.

TRACK STATS

- **Shape**: Road course
- **Seating**: 120,000
- **Length**: 3.41 miles (5.5 km)
- **Location**: Austin, Texas

NASCAR track circuit
Alternative track or pit road

The Circuit of the Americas is the first racetrack in the US to be built specifically for F1.

DARLINGTON RACEWAY

Darlington Raceway opened in 1950, making NASCAR's first real superspeedway. It is considered NASCAR's most difficult track and has earned the nickname "Too Tough to Tame." The track is an important part of NASCAR's heritage and home to the Southern 500 race.

TRACK STATS

- **Shape**: Oval
- **Seating**: 47,000
- **Length**: 1.366 miles (2.2 km)
- **Location**: Darlington, South Carolina

NASCAR track circuit
Pit road

The Darlington Raceway was built in the shape of an egg to avoid a minnow pond at one end.

DAYTONA INTERNATIONAL SPEEDWAY

Known as the "World Center of Racing," the Daytona International Speedway hosts the iconic Daytona 500, NASCAR's most prestigious race. The track's banking is steep, challenging drivers to be at their best at high speeds. The track opened in 1959, and the first Daytona 500 took place that same year.

The speedway hosts other motorsports events, such as motorcycle races, as well as concerts, car shows, and vehicle testing.

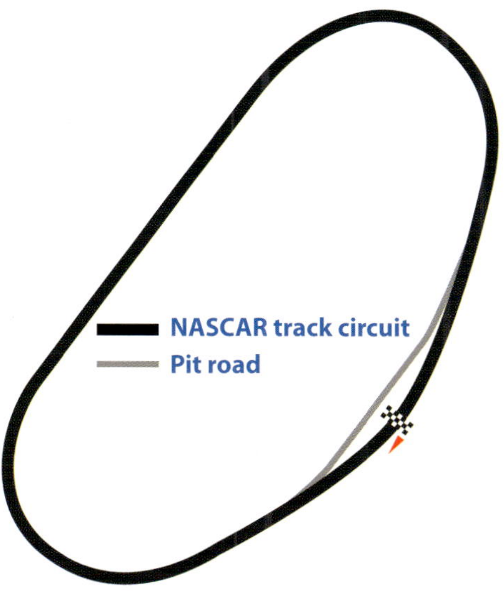

The Daytona International Speedway is also the home of the Motorsports Hall of Fame of America.

TRACK STATS

- **Shape**: Tri-oval
- **Seating**: 101,500
- **Length**: 2.5 miles (4 km)
- **Location**: Daytona Beach, Florida

DOVER MOTOR SPEEDWAY

TRACK STATS

- **Shape**: Oval
- **Seating**: 85,000
- **Length**: 1 mile (1.6 km)
- **Location**: Dover, Delaware

NASCAR track circuit
Alternative track or pit road

Dover Motor Speedway is known as the "Monster Mile" due to its concrete surface and high-banked turns. This track has been in the NASCAR circuit since 1969.

Dover Motor Speedway

TRACK STATS

- **Shape**: Oval (dirt track)
- **Seating**: 30,000
- **Length**: 0.5 miles (0.8 km)
- **Location**: Rossburg, Ohio

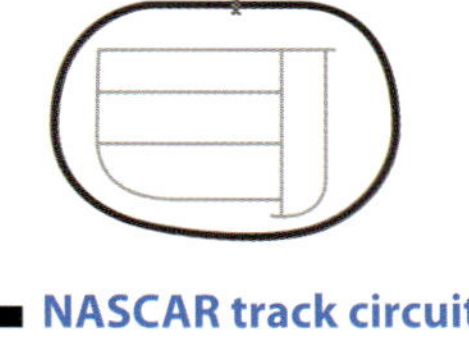

NASCAR track circuit
Alternative track or pit road

ELDORA SPEEDWAY

Eldora Speedway is one of few dirt tracks that host NASCAR races. The dirt track helps bring NASCAR fans back the roots of racing. The track was built on what used to be a large cornfield.

Homestead-Miami Speedway

HOMESTEAD-MIAMI SPEEDWAY

Homestead-Miami Speedway has been a part of NASCAR's modern era since 1995. The track has two tunnels underneath it. Race cars, support vehicles, and crews use them to get to the raceway.

NASCAR IN THE KNOW

Except for road courses, NASCAR races always run counterclockwise. There are several possible reasons why. Some say the tradition is based on horse racing, which also runs counterclockwise. Others think it's because turning left is easier for right-handed people, who make up the majority of the population. Left turns are also safer for the driver, who has a better view of the track and can stay farther away from the wall.

TRACK STATS

- **Shape**: Oval
- **Seating**: 46,000
- **Length**: 1.5 miles (2.4 km)
- **Location**: Homestead, Florida

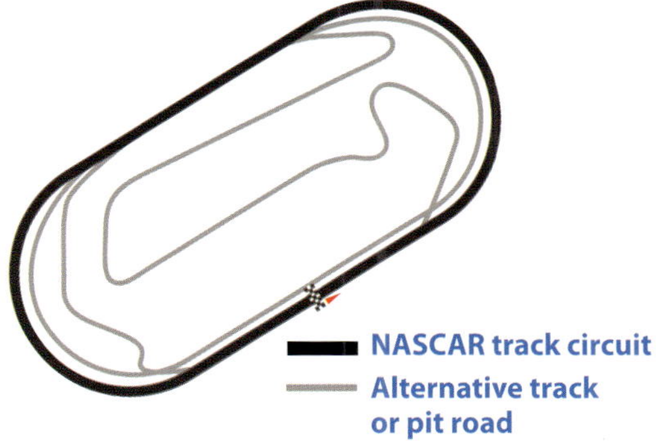

INDIANAPOLIS MOTOR SPEEDWAY

Indianapolis Motor Speedway is an iconic NASCAR track. It has hosted the Brickyard 400 since 1994. The track's history dates back to 1909. When it was first built, the track was made of bricks—more than 3 million of them. It's also home to the "kissing the bricks" tradition, making it a special place in NASCAR.

TRACK STATS

- **Shape**: Oval
- **Seating**: 257,000
- **Length**: 2.5 miles (4 km)
- **Location**: Indianapolis, Indiana

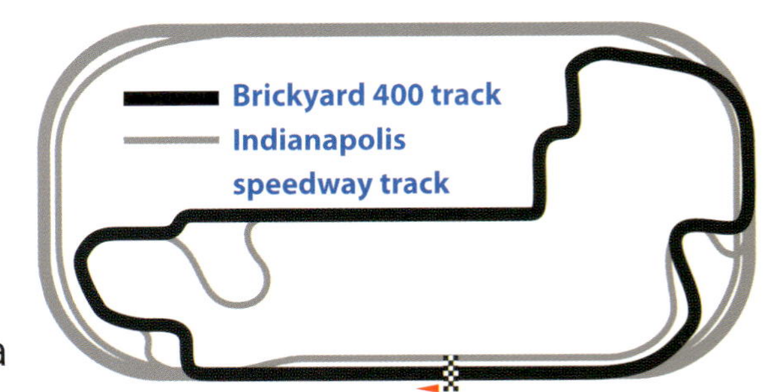

The Indianapolis Motor Speedway is the first racing facility to use the term "Speedway."

NASCAR IN THE KNOW

The tradition of "kissing the bricks" started in 1996 by Dale Jarrett after he won the Brickyard 400. It was a way to honor the history of the Indianapolis Motor Speedway. Since then, each winner of the Brickyard 400 has followed the tradition.

LAS VEGAS MOTOR SPEEDWAY

Las Vegas Motor Speedway has been a hub for NASCAR since 1996. It's home to races such as the Pennzoil 400 and is known for its energetic atmosphere. It's a top destination for NASCAR fans from across the country.

TRACK STATS

- **Shape**: Tri-oval
- **Seating**: 123,000
- **Length**: 1.5 miles (2.4 km)
- **Location**: Las Vegas, Nevada

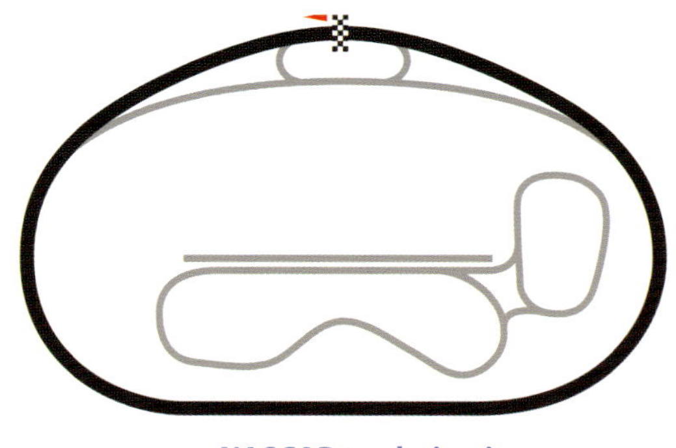

The Las Vegas Motor Speedway has nine different tracks for a variety of racing.

NASCAR IN THE KNOW

Imagine getting a huge grandfather clock as a trophy. That's what winners receive at the Martinsville Speedway in Virginia! The clock was first given as a trophy in 1964. The owner of the speedway, H. Clay Earles, wanted a trophy that wouldn't just collect dust.

MARTINSVILLE SPEEDWAY

Martinsville Speedway has been in continuous use since 1947 and is known for its paper clip shape. It hosts the Martinsville 500, known for tight, close-quarters racing. The historic track's iconic grandfather clock trophy makes it a treasured part of NASCAR tradition.

TRACK STATS

- **Shape**: Oval
- **Seating**: 60,000
- **Length**: 0.526 miles (0.8 km)
- **Location**: Ridgeway, Virginia

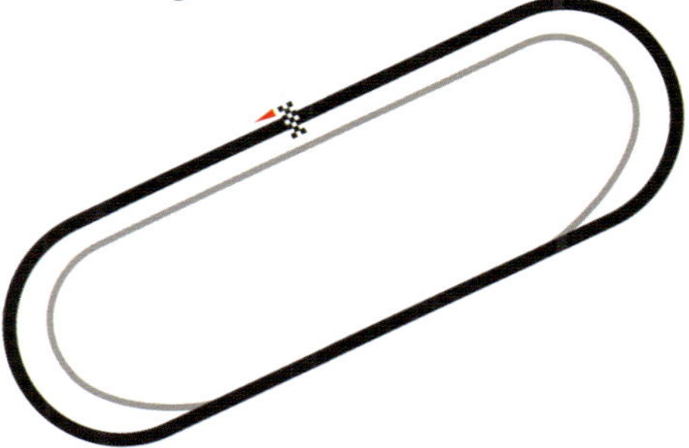

NASCAR track circuit
Alternative track or pit road

Michigan International Speedway

MICHIGAN INTERNATIONAL SPEEDWAY

This 2-mile (3.2-km) speedway has been hosting races for more than 50 years. Turns along this track are 73 feet (22 m) wide, challenging every driver that races here. The track holds more than 50,000 people and is surrounded with greenery and lakes.

TRACK STATS

- **Shape**: D-shaped oval
- **Seating**: 56,000
- **Length**: 2 miles (3.2 km)
- **Location**: Brooklyn, Michigan

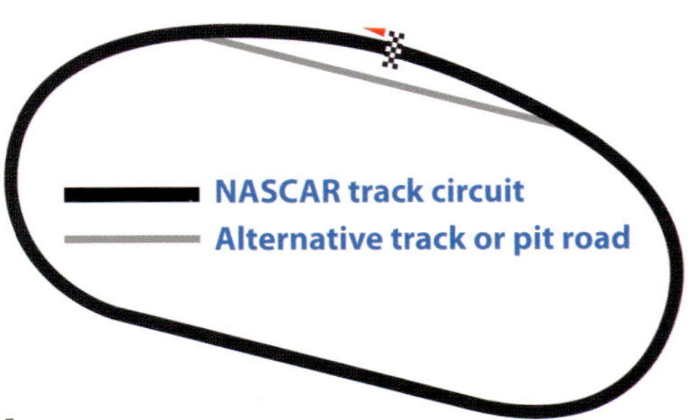

NASHVILLE SUPERSPEEDWAY

Nashville Superspeedway rejoined the NASCAR schedule in 2021. It is known for its challenging concrete track. It hosts the Cup Series Ally 400 race and can accommodate 25,000 fans.

TRACK STATS

- **Shape**: D-shaped oval
- **Seating**: 25,000
- **Length**: 1.33 miles (2.1 km)
- **Location**: Lebanon, Tennessee

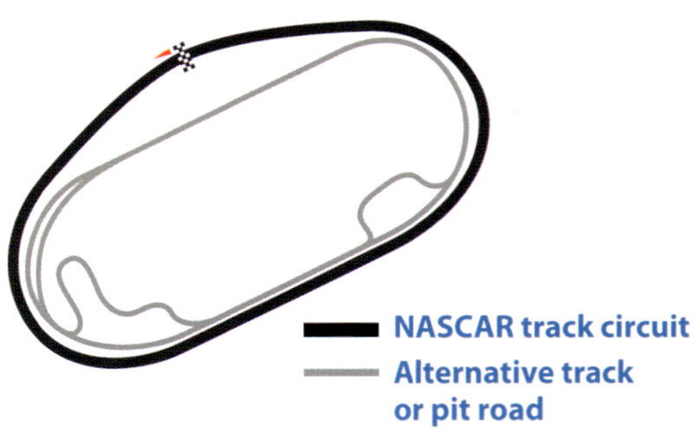

PHOENIX RACEWAY

Cale Yarborough won his first NASCAR Winston West Series race at the Phoenix Raceway in 1977. The track was struck by lightning in 1987, and most of it burned to the ground. It was soon rebuilt and continues to host NASCAR races today.

TRACK STATS

- **Shape**: Oval
- **Seating**: 42,000
- **Length**: 1 mile (1.6 km)
- **Location**: Avondale, Arizona

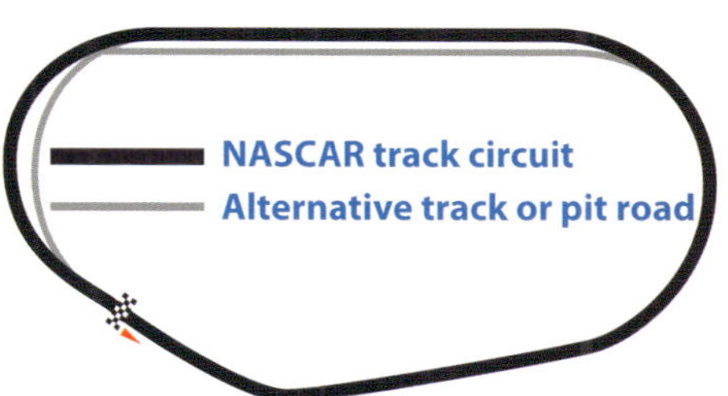

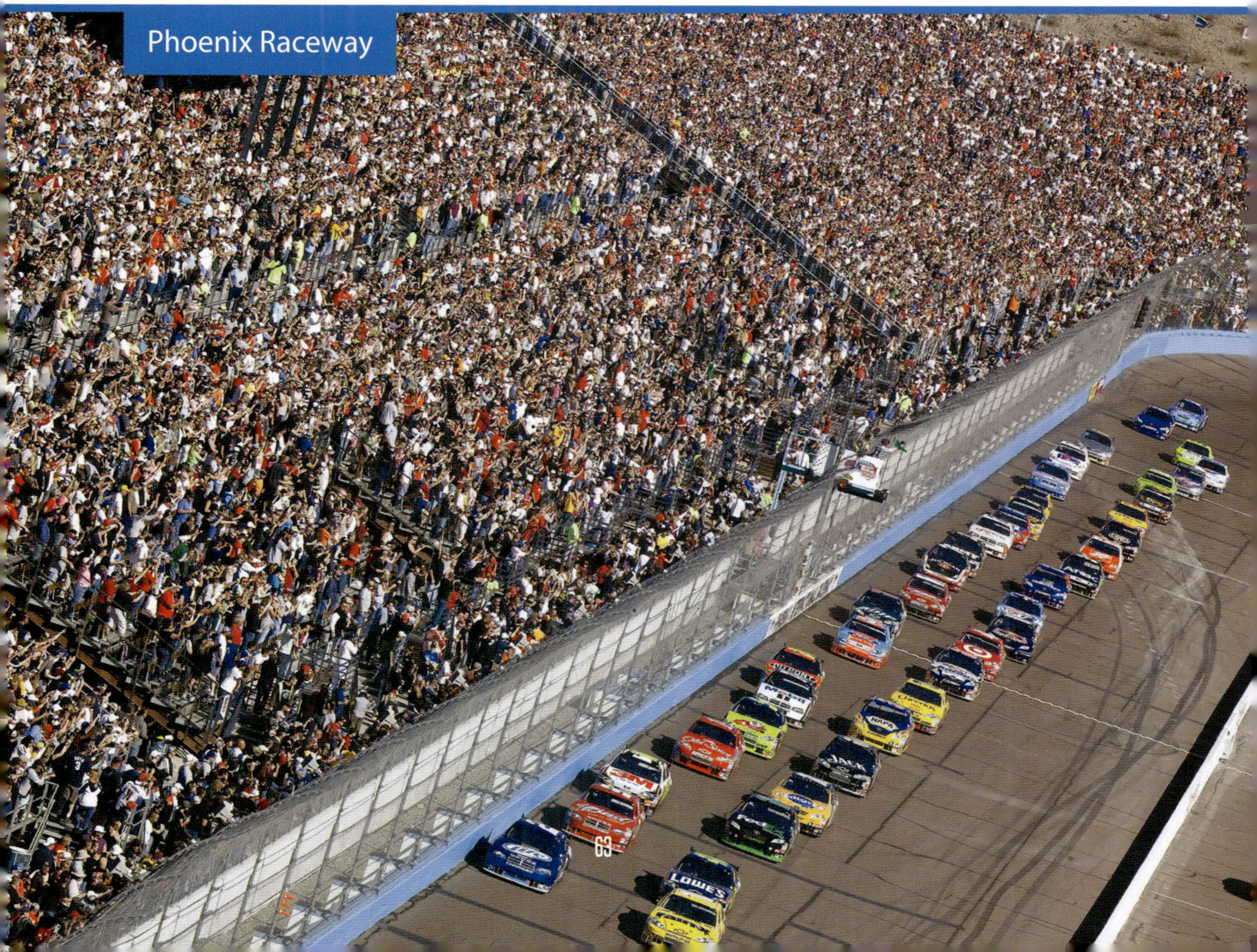

Phoenix Raceway

POCONO RACEWAY

The shape of the Pocono Raceway is called a triangular oval because the track has three sharp turns. It has hosted NASCAR races since 1974, including the Pocono 350. The Pocono Raceway is not only a fun and challenging track, but it's also located in a beautiful place.

TRACK STATS

- **Shape**: Triangular oval
- **Seating**: 76,812
- **Length**: 2.5 miles (4 km)
- **Location**: Long Pond, Pennsylvania

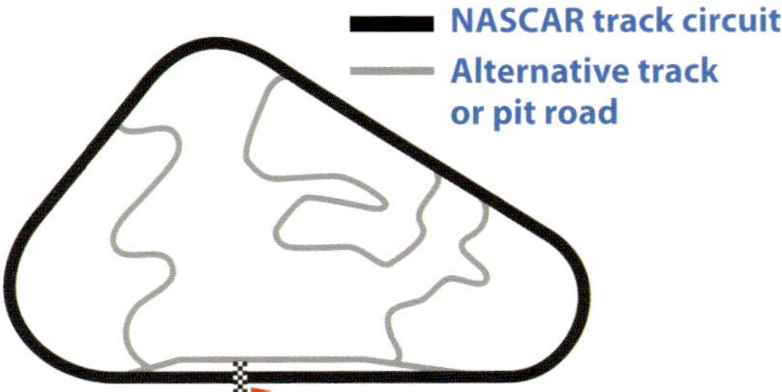

RICHMOND RACEWAY

Richmond Raceway is a short track with a long history. It has been part of the NASCAR circuit since 1953. It is home to the Federated Auto Parts 400 race, and the track is known for being particularly tight, making it hard for cars to break away from others on the track.

Richmond Raceway originally had a dirt track.

TRACK STATS

- **Shape**: Oval
- **Seating**: 51,000
- **Length**: 0.75 miles (1.2 km)
- **Location**: Richmond, Virginia

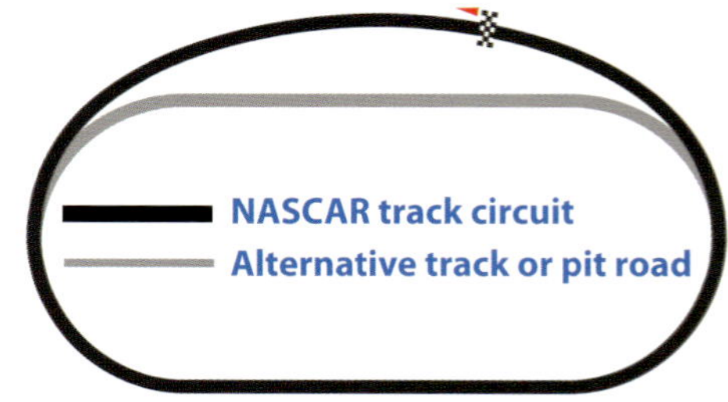

The Road America track is known for its challenging corners.

ROAD AMERICA

In 2021, the Road America track was named the best NASCAR track in the United States by *USA Today*. It first hosted a NASCAR race in August 1956. This was before the organization had grown to race all across the country.

NASCAR IN THE KNOW

Before a race begins, drivers will drive their cars slowly and swerve back and forth. This warms up the tires and clears off the marbles.

TRACK STATS

- **Shape**: Road course
- **Seating**: 150,000
- **Length**: 4 miles (6.4 km)
- **Location**: Elkhart Lake, Wisconsin

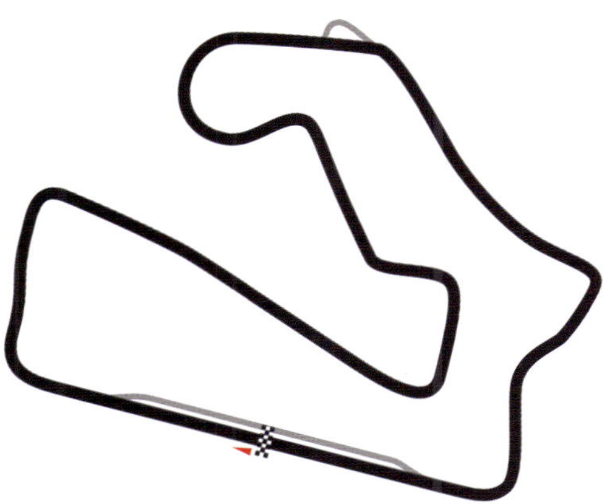

NASCAR track circuit
Alternative track or pit road

SONOMA RACEWAY

The Sonoma Raceway is known for its twists and turns. The track is also hilly and has an elevation change of 160 feet (49 m). This challenging track has been on the NASCAR circuit since 1989.

Sonoma Raceway is located in Sonoma, California, which is famous for its vineyards and wine industry. Winners at Sonoma drink wine from a special goblet as part of the raceway's traditions.

TRACK STATS

- **Shape**: Road course
- **Seating**: 47,000
- **Length**: 2.5 miles (4 km)
- **Location**: Sonoma, California

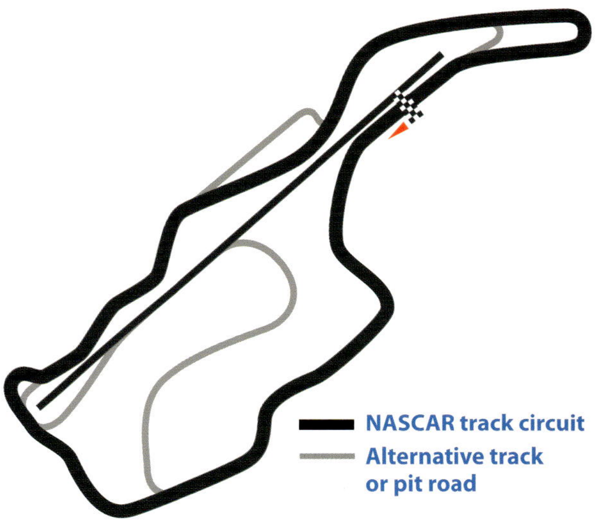

Sonoma Raceway was built on land that was once a farm.

TEXAS MOTOR SPEEDWAY

The Texas Motor Speedway is known for its high banks and for being one of the world's largest racing venues. It can hold about 200,000 people! The track is home to NASCAR's All-Star Race. NASCAR legends Terry and Bobby Labonte and Jeff Gordon helped break ground on the track in 1995.

TRACK STATS

- **Shape**: Oval
- **Seating**: 200,000
- **Length**: 1.5 miles (2.4 km)
- **Location**: Fort Worth, Texas

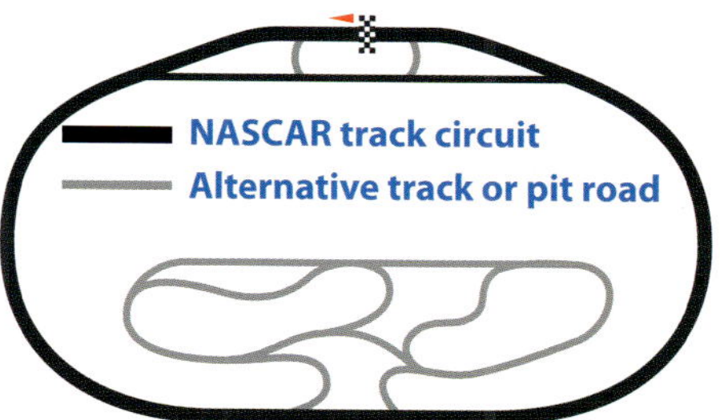

NASCAR IN THE KNOW

Pace cars lead race cars around the track at the beginning of a race, setting the speed for the initial laps to help drivers warm up their engines and tires. In the case of an accident or bad weather, a pace car comes out, and the race cars follow it at a reduced speed until the situation is cleared.

Pace cars are an important safety feature in NASCAR.

The Talladega Superspeedway is NASCAR's longest and fastest track.

TALLADEGA SUPERSPEEDWAY

The Talladega Superspeedway is a historic track that opened in 1969. It was built on what was once a soybean farm. The track is home to two NASCAR Cup Series races, including the Geico 500. This track holds lots of fans: more than 175,000. It is also where legendary

TRACK STATS

- **Shape**: Tri-oval
- **Seating**: 80,000
- **Length**: 2.7 miles (4.3 km)
- **Location**: Talladega, Alabama

NASCAR track circuit
pit road

FUN FACT

The movie *Talladega Nights: The Ballad of Ricky Bobby* is a comedy about NASCAR and the Talladega Superspeedway.

driver Buddy Baker became the first racer to make a turn at more than 200 miles per hour (322 kmh).

NASCAR IN THE KNOW

After cars have finished racing in NASCAR, some get sold to other racing organizations or to collectors. Some are displayed at car shows. Others are donated to racing teams that are developing their skills, and some cars are sent to the junkyard after any useful parts are taken out.

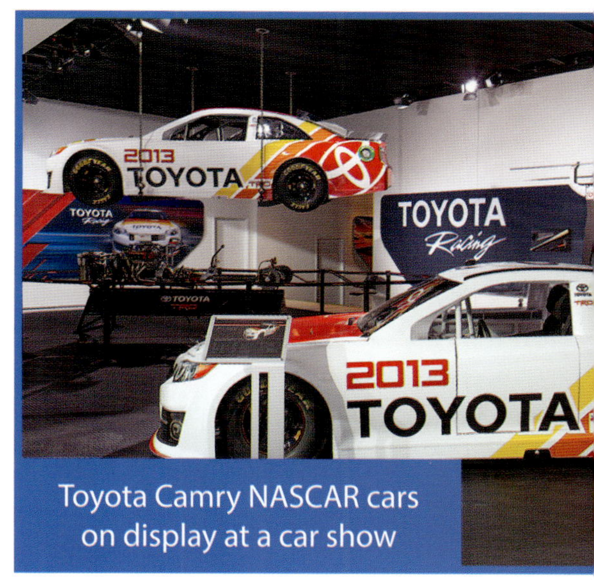

Toyota Camry NASCAR cars on display at a car show

PIT STOPS

Pit stops are a critical part of stock car racing. During a pit stop, race cars pull off the track for essential maintenance, refueling, and adjustments. This allows drivers to optimize their car's performance without losing too much time during the race. The pit crew is a group of highly skilled professionals, trained to perform maintenance on a race car in record time.

NASCAR IN THE KNOW

In the Daytona 500, each car is limited to 15 sets of tires, or 60 individual tires.

GASMAN: refuels the car

On average, it takes about 12 seconds to change all four tires and refuel the car during a pit stop.

THE DAYTONA 500

The Daytona 500 is called "The Great American Race."

Football has the Super Bowl, hockey has the Stanley Cup, and baseball has the World Series. In NASCAR, the Daytona 500 is considered the most popular and important race. What makes the Daytona 500 different is that it kicks off the NASCAR racing season. Other sports, like football, end with their biggest events.

The Daytona 500 takes place every February at the Daytona International Speedway. It is more than just a race—it is a multiweek

BY THE NUMBERS:

First year: 1959
Miles: 500
Laps: 200
Most wins by a driver: 7, Richard Petty
Most wins by a team: 9, Petty Enterprises
Number of people who attend: more than 100,000
Number of people who watch on television: more than 10 million

event. The two weeks leading up to the race are called Speedweeks. Fans come from all over to enjoy the festivities, special events, prerace competitions and practices, and meet and greets with drivers. Tailgating and camping have become fan favorites. Camping passes allow fans to park their recreational vehicles (RVs), set up tents, and pull camping trailers into the infield. Not only can fans stay in the infield overnight, but they can also watch the race from there too.

A win at the Daytona 500 is not only prestigious, but it also comes with the largest purse of any NASCAR race. In 2023, the winning team was paid almost $30 million!

Dale Earnhardt Jr. wins the Daytona 500 in 2014.

OTHER BIG NASCAR RACES

- Coca-Cola 600 (Charlotte Motor Speedway)
- NASCAR All-Star Race (location varies)
- Geico 500 (Talladega Superspeedway)
- NASCAR Championship Race (Phoenix Raceway)
- Pocono 400 (Pocono Raceway)
- Bristol Night Race (Bristol Motor Speedway)

WOMEN IN NASCAR

ALBA COLON

Alba Colon studied engineering at the University of Puerto Rico. After graduation, she headed a team of engineers to build race cars from the ground up. Her career as an engineer in the racing industry continued to advance, and by 2001, she was working for General Motors' NASCAR Cup Series program. In 2018, Colon became the director for competition systems for NASCAR's Hendrick Motorsports team.

JANET GUTHRIE

Before becoming a race car driver, Janet Guthrie was a flight instructor and an aerospace engineer. Guthrie became interested in racing after buying a sports car and began competing in races

FUN FACT

Janet Guthrie's racing helmet and driver's suit are at the Smithsonian Museum in Washington, DC.

for the Sports Car Club of America. In 1972, she became the first woman to compete in a NASCAR premier superspeedway race. In 1977, she was the first woman to qualify and compete in the Daytona 500. She also raced in the Indianapolis 500. In 2023, Guthrie was awarded the NASCAR Hall of Fame Landmark Award for Outstanding Contributions to NASCAR.

ASHLEY PARLETT

Ashley Parlett became hooked on racing at 11 years old. She asked her father for a go-kart. But, in order to race, he wanted her to learn how to repair it. She did, and she enjoyed working on cars into her 20s. She got an internship to work on trucks in NASCAR's Truck Series. By 2007, she was a car chief. Her job was to get the race car set up properly for the crew chief.

NASCAR FLAGS

Flags play an important role in NASCAR. They are a way to quickly communicate to drivers. There are many different flags in NASCAR racing, and each one means something different.

- **Black flag:** a driver must leave the track
- **Black flag with crossed white lines:** driver isn't following instructions to go to the pit, usually resulting in disqualification
- **Blue flag:** track conditions are normal, but it is hard to see any problems ahead
- **Blue flag with yellow diagonal stripe:** leaders are approaching a lapped driver

- **Checkered flag (black and white):** the race has ended
- **Checkered flag (green):** the race stage has ended
- **Green flag:** start the race, track conditions are normal
- **Red and black flags together:** it is the end of practice or the qualifying session
- **Red flag:** halt the race
- **Two checkered flags together:** the race has reached the halfway point
- **White flag:** one lap left in the race
- **Yellow flag:** race with caution

In the United States, NASCAR has a long and strong history, and with that come numerous traditions.

PRE-RACE CEREMONIES

It is custom at all NASCAR races to do a few things before a race begins. First, there is a salute to the United States military. Then a prayer is given for the drivers along with the singing of the national anthem. Once these traditions are complete, the grand marshal asks drivers to start their engines! Many times, a celebrity, rather than the grand marshal, will be chosen to make this famous announcement.

Air Force Senior Master Sergeant Ryan Carson sings "America the Beautiful" at a prerace ceremony at Homestead-Miami Speedway.

HAULER PARADE

Numerous NASCAR races hold a hauler parade before the big event. Haulers are the huge semitrucks that carry race cars from place to place. During a parade, the haulers line up and drive down local streets while fans wave from the sidelines. The trucks showcase

Bubba Wallace signs an autograph.

different drivers and cars, depending on which driver's car they are carrying.

SPEEDWEEKS AT DAYTONA

Every year, NASCAR kicks off the racing season with Speedweeks in Daytona. It's a two-week celebration that ends with the Daytona 500. During Speedweeks, fans can watch drivers practice and qualify for pole positions. They can also meet and greet drivers. There are many events throughout the two weeks of Speedweeks.

FUN FACT

Before a race begins, drivers take a qualifying lap. The driver with the fastest speed gets the best position in the main race. This is known as the pole position.

CHAMPAGNE CELEBRATIONS

There are lots of ways drivers celebrate a victory, but nearly all NASCAR wins end with champagne being sprayed on the driver and their team.

POLISH VICTORY LAPS

Former NASCAR driver Alan Kulwicki saluted fans by driving a *clockwise* victory lap, opposite of how the race is run, after winning his first race. He did the same after two later victories. Tragically, Kulwicki died in a plane crash in 1993. After his passing, other NASCAR drivers began doing his victory laps in honor of Kulwicki. The laps then became a way to honor

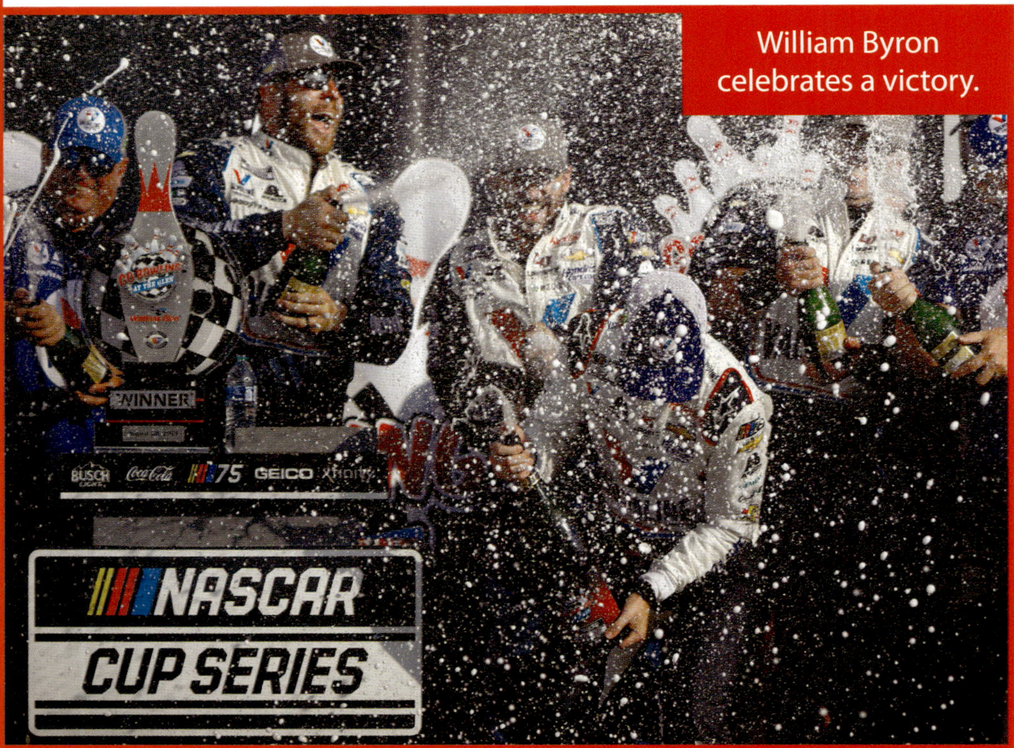

William Byron celebrates a victory.

Many NASCAR winners hop back into their cars after the race to do a burnout while the fans cheer.

others. NASCAR driver Kevin Harvick did a lap in honor of Dale Earnhardt Sr. after his death. The laps are called "Polish" in reference to Alan Kulwicki's ancestry.

NASCAR IN THE KNOW

There are many traditions in racing outside of NASCAR. After the Indianapolis 500, an open-wheeled race, the winner chugs down a glass of milk! The tradition began in 1936 when the winner, Louis Meyer, gulped down a glass of buttermilk at the end of the race. Ever since then, winners have kept up the tradition.

BURNOUTS

Burnouts have become another NASCAR celebration tradition. A burnout is when a driver spins the tires while moving the car as little as possible. This creates lots of smoke, noise, and black tire patterns on the track.

YOUTH AND RACING

Many professional race car drivers started racing as children. Kids have a variety of avenues to explore racing, from go-karts to specialized cars.

Go-kart racing

GO-KART RACING

Go-karts are mini race cars built for kids. They provide an exciting entry point into motorsports. Indoor tracks offer competitive go-kart racing where friends can race one another, learning the

NASCAR IN THE KNOW

There are many types of safety gear to keep young racers safe. Helmets and race suits might be obvious, but there are a few items that might be surprising.

- Long boots provide ankle support but are still flexible so the drivers can move their feet on the pedals.
- Fire-resistant underwear and socks help prevent burns in the case of an accident.
- A rib protector protects a driver's chest from impact.
- Gloves provide grip on a car's steering wheel and protect the hands from injury in the case of a fire.

Quarter midget racing

basics of racing. It's a safe, fun way to develop driving skills and a love for motorsports.

QUARTER MIDGET RACING

Quarter midgets are scaled-down race cars suitable for kids as young as age five. A quarter midget track is short and designed for younger racers, making it a perfect place for kids to start racing. They gain fundamental skills and form connections in the racing community.

JUNIOR DRAG RACING

Junior drag racing focuses on speed, with kids and teens racing in straight-line sprints. The tracks are specially designed for safety. Junior drag racing is often an avenue into high-speed competition.

Junior drag racing

FANS

One of the most popular sports in the United States, NASCAR has a long history of loyal fans. With that comes a large fan culture that is strong and thriving.

One of the most popular traditions among fans is tailgating. Fans arrive hours early to a race, park their cars, and spend time together—talking, eating, and enjoying the anticipation of the main event. Some fans even arrive the night before the race to get a good spot for their tailgate party!

Fans have their favorite drivers and teams, and they can't wait to meet the stars of the show. Meet and greets, like FanZones and FanFests, are also a major part of the NASCAR fan culture. Before a race begins, there are often autograph signings, time to speak with drivers and ask questions, and take pictures. Fans can also take part in pit walks—a chance to see a race pit and what happens

Clint Bowyer is introduced at the Charlotte Motor Speedway.

behind-the-scenes of these intense races. Social media has become another way for fans to interact with drivers and for drivers to connect with fans.

FUN FACT

NASCAR is known as one of the most fan-friendly sports.

BOBBY ALLISON

With 84 wins over a 25-year career, Bobby Allison is an iconic figure in NASCAR. He won the Daytona 500 three times: in 1978, 1982, and 1988. Allison also won the prestigious 1983 Winston Cup championship. Just a few months after his last Daytona win, Allison was in a dangerous crash. He retired after the accident but went on to become a race car owner.

Bobby Allison was part of a group of drivers known as the Alabama Gang.

DRIVER STATS

- **Years Raced**: 1961 to 1988
- **Wins**: 84
- **Awards**: Premier Series champion, 1983; named one of NASCAR's 50 Greatest Drivers; NASCAR Hall of Fame, inducted 2011

DAVEY ALLISON

Davey Allison was the son of racing legend Bobby Allison, but he made his own way as a driver with 19 wins in the Cup Series, including the 1992 Daytona 500. He was on his way to a championship, but he died in a helicopter crash in July 1993.

DRIVER STATS

- **Years Raced**: 1985 to 1993
- **Wins**: 19
- **Awards**: Rookie of the Year, 1987; named one of NASCAR's 50 Greatest Drivers; NASCAR Hall of Fame, inducted 2019

DONNIE ALLISON

Donnie Allison, Bobby's younger brother, won Rookie of the Year in 1967 and went on to win a number of races. But Donnie might be best known for a scuffle he had with fellow driver Cale Yarborough at the 1979 Daytona 500. The two drivers crashed and were out of the race. Each blamed the other for the wreck. It was the first NASCAR race on live television, and their fight made major news across the country.

DRIVER STATS

- **Years Raced**: 1966 to 1988
- **Wins**: 10
- **Awards**: Rookie of the Year, 1967; named one of NASCAR's 50 Greatest Drivers; NASCAR Hall of Fame, inducted 2024

Donnie Allison and Cale Yarborough crash into each other at the 1979 Daytona 500.

BUCK BAKER

Buck Baker

Buck Baker was a bus driver before becoming a racer. He was also a bootlegger. He made and sold alcohol when it was illegal in the United States. His bootlegging brought him to racing, which he started doing in the 1940s. Baker joined NASCAR in its first year and became a star driver. In his 27-year career, he had 46 wins. After leaving NASCAR, Baker opened numerous racing schools. He taught famous drivers such as Jeff Gordon and Bobby Hillin.

DRIVER STATS

- **Years Raced**: 1949 to 1976
- **Wins**: 46
- **Awards**: Winner of two consecutive championships, 1956 and 1957; named one of NASCAR's 50 Greatest Drivers; NASCAR Hall of Fame, inducted 2024

FUN FACT

Buck Baker was the first NASCAR driver to win two consecutive premier series championships, in 1956 and 1957.

BUDDY BAKER

In 1980, Buddy Baker won the Daytona 500 at the fastest speed on record: 177.603 miles per hour (285.8 kmh). Before that historic race, Baker had already won victories at the South 500 and Darlington Raceways as well as two World 600 races. When he started driving for NASCAR in 1959, his father Buck was racing too. Buddy was a master at racing on NASCAR's fastest tracks, Daytona and Talladega, and he still holds the record for all-time lap leader at the Talladega Speedway with 1,099 laps led.

Buddy Baker

DRIVER STATS

- **Years Raced**: 1959 to 1992
- **Wins**: 19
- **Awards**: Named one of NASCAR's 50 Greatest Drivers; NASCAR Hall of Fame, inducted 2020

NEIL BONNETT

Neil Bonnett's career in racing took him to the big screen: he was in two Hollywood movies. Bonnett began in the racing world as a mechanic. He worked on Bobby Allison's cars. Soon, he switched gears and became a driver. Though he only raced in five full-time seasons, he won 18 Cup races. In 1982 and 1983, he won back-to-back races at the Coca-Cola 600 race. When not racing, Bonnett made television appearances as a NASCAR commentator.

DRIVER STATS

- **Years Raced**: 1973 to 1994
- **Wins**: 18
- **Awards**: Named one of NASCAR's 50 Greatest Drivers; nominated for the NASCAR Hall of Fame

FUN FACT

Neil Bonnett appeared in the 1983 film *Stroker Ace* and the 1990 film *Days of Thunder.*

Neil Bonnett at the 1982 Daytona 500

Jeff Burton signs autographs at a Winston Cup race.

JEFF BURTON

Jeff Burton is one of only 10 drivers to have at least 20 wins in two different NASCAR series: 21 Cup Series wins and 27 Xfinity Series wins. In 1997, he won his first Cup Series race at the Texas Motor Speedway. His best year in racing was 1999, winning six races, including the Coca-Cola 600 and the Southern 500. Over his career, Burton earned the nickname "The Mayor." He was always thinking about how to improve the sport.

DRIVER STATS

- **Years Raced**: 1993 to 2014
- **Wins**: 21
- **Awards**: Rookie of the Year, 1994; named one of NASCAR's 50 Greatest Drivers; nominated for the NASCAR Hall of Fame

NASCAR IN THE KNOW

In 2000, Jeff Burton became one of only two drivers in NASCAR history who have led every lap in a race. The only other driver to do so was Cale Yarborough, who accomplished this feat two times, first in 1973 and again in 1978.

KURT BUSCH

As a child, Kurt Busch attended races with his father and developed a love for the sport. Busch started his NASCAR career in what is now the NASCAR Truck Series. He raced for seven different NASCAR teams and drove in 776 NASCAR Cup Series races throughout his career. He was a winner of the Daytona 500. In July 2022, Busch suffered a concussion after an accident at the Pocono Raceway. Though he was hoping to return to racing, he decided to retire.

Kurt Busch drove for NASCAR for 23 years.

DRIVER STATS

- **Years Raced**: 1999 to 2022
- **Wins**: 34
- **Awards**: NASCAR Truck Series Rookie of the Year, 2000; Cup Series champion, 2004; Indianapolis 500 Rookie of the Year, 2014

Red Byron, Daytona Beach, 1948

ROBERT NOLD "RED" BYRON

Born in 1915, Robert "Red" Byron was a pioneer of car racing. He became the first-ever person to win a race on the Daytona Beach Road Course in 1948. The same year, he won NASCAR's first championship, the Strictly Stock. It would later become known as the Cup Series. Byron's car, number 22, had his name painted on it.

DRIVER STATS

- **Years Raced**: 1949 to 1951
- **Wins**: 2
- **Awards**: NASCAR's first season champion; NASCAR Hall of Fame, inducted 2018

NASCAR IN THE KNOW

Safety is a top priority for NASCAR. Drivers wear suits made with fire-retardant material, which is also woven into their socks, shoes, underwear, and gloves. The crew wears the clothing to protect themselves in case of a fire during a pit stop. Helmets also contain fire-retardant material and are built to keep a driver's head stable at high speeds. NASCAR helmets cover the entire head, and most also cover the face, protecting a driver from flying debris. Some drivers choose to wear open-face helmets and use goggles for eye protection.

SARA CHRISTIAN

Sara Christian was the first female driver in NASCAR history. She was also the first and only woman to compete in NASCAR's first race at the Charlotte Speedway in 1949. She placed 13th driving her husband's Ford. Christian's second race was at the Daytona Beach Road Course in July 1949. The race included two other women: Ethel Mobley and Louise Smith. In October 1949, Sara finished fifth at the Heidelberg Raceway in Pennsylvania. Her fifth and 13th place finishes are still the best for a woman in NASCAR's top series.

DRIVER STATS

- **Years Raced**: 1949 to 1950
- **Wins**: 0 (2 top tens)
- **Awards**: United States Drivers Association Woman Driver of the Year, 1949; Georgia Racing Hall of Fame, inducted 2004

Sara Christian in the early 1950s

DALE EARNHARDT JR.

Dale Earnhardt Jr. has racing in his blood. His father, Dale Earnhardt Sr., was a NASCAR legend. Earnhardt Jr. first raced for NASCAR part time in 1996 on his father's team. By 1998, he won his first championship, and he soon moved up to NASCAR's top series. His star was on the rise, but 2001 was a tragic year. Earnhardt Sr. died in a crash during the Daytona 500. Earnhardt Jr. continued racing until 2017, carrying on his family's legacy. He is one of the most popular NASCAR drivers of all time.

Dale Earnhardt Jr. at the Richmond International Raceway

DRIVER STATS

- **Years Raced**: 1998 to 2017
- **Wins**: 26
- **Awards**: 15 "Most Popular Driver" awards; Xfinity Series champion, 1998 and 1999; NASCAR Hall of Fame, inducted 2021

FUN FACT

Dale Earnhardt Jr. is a five-time NASCAR champion.

DALE EARNHARDT SR.

Dale Earnhardt Sr. started racing as a teenager after borrowing money to buy and fix old cars. He was determined to make it in the racing world. In 1975, he made his stock car racing debut at the World 600 race at the Charlotte Motor Speedway.

In 1979, he was offered a spot on a NASCAR team. He won his first race at the Southeastern 500 Speedway in Bristol, Tennessee. Later that year, he earned the title Rookie of the Year after making the top ten 17 times. In 1980, Earnhardt Sr. won his first championship. He was the first driver to win Rookie of the Year and a championship back-to-back.

Earnhardt Sr. broke record after record throughout his career. By

Many consider Dale Earnhardt Sr. to be the most famous NASCAR driver of all time.

Dale Earnhardt Jr. and Dale Earnhardt Sr. at the Darlington Raceway

1994, he had won seven Winston Cup Series championships. In 1996, he became the first driver to start in 500 consecutive Winston Cup races. But he wanted to win the crown jewel of NASCAR races: the Daytona 500.

In 1997, Earnhardt Sr. survived a dangerous crash and returned to racing the following year, winning the 1998 Daytona 500. Just three years later, tragedy struck. Earnhardt Sr. crashed his car during the 2001 Daytona 500 while trying to help his son, Earnhardt Jr., and another driver keep their leads. He was hit from behind and struck a wall. He died on impact. Today, Dale Earnhardt Sr. is remembered as one of the best drivers in NASCAR history.

DRIVER STATS

- **Years Raced**: 1975 to 2001
- **Wins**: 76
- **Awards**: Rookie of the Year, 1979; Winner of seven NASCAR championships; NASCAR Hall of Fame, inducted 2010

FUN FACT

Dale Earnhardt Sr. was known as "The Intimidator."

Carl Edwards celebrates a win at Texas Motor Speedway.

CARL EDWARDS

Carl Edwards had a bit of a different path to the racetrack. He started out as a substitute teacher while trying to make his way as a race car driver. He handed out business cards to anyone in the business in an effort to get noticed, and it worked. Soon, Edwards was racing in the Cup Series. One of his most notable races came in 2011 when he lost the championship title in a tiebreaker.

DRIVER STATS

- **Years Raced**: 2004 to 2016
- **Wins**: 28
- **Awards**: NASCAR Hall of Fame nominee

Bill Elliott in 2018

BILL ELLIOTT

Bill Elliott raced for NASCAR for 37 years. Elliott started in 1976, and it was a bumpy ride at first. But by 1983, his career took off. Elliott won the Daytona 500 in 1985 and 1987, and he earned the nickname "Million Dollar Bill" after winning the Daytona 500, Winston 500, and Southern 500 in the same year. He received $1 million for the three wins.

FUN FACT

Bill Elliot was given the nickname "Awesome Bill from Dawsonville," a nod to his Georgia hometown.

DRIVER STATS

- **Years Raced**: 1976 to 2012
- **Wins**: 44
- **Awards**: 16 "Most Popular Driver" awards; NASCAR Cup champion, 1988; NASCAR Hall of Fame, inducted 2015

Tim Flock won the Daytona Beach convertible race in 1957.

TIM FLOCK

Tim Flock's 18 wins in the 1955 NASCAR racing season was a record for the most wins in one season. It held for 12 years until Richard Petty broke it in 1967. Flock had many jobs before he made it big in NASCAR. Among them, he served in the military, was a cab driver, and was a bootlegger—bringing whiskey into Georgia at a time when it was illegal. Flock won 21 percent of his races in NASCAR's premier series, one of the highest records in NASCAR history.

NASCAR IN THE KNOW

For Tim Flock, racing was a family affair. He and all of his siblings raced for NASCAR in the early years, including his sister Ethel. She was one of NASCAR's first female drivers. The Flocks hold a record for most siblings to drive in the same premier series race. The record has held since 1949.

DRIVER STATS

- **Years Raced**: 1949 to 1961
- **Wins**: 39
- **Awards**: Named one of NASCAR's 50 Greatest Drivers; NASCAR Cup champion, 1952 and 1955; NASCAR Hall of Fame, inducted 2014

A. J. FOYT

A. J. Foyt is the only NASCAR driver to ever win the Daytona 500, the Indianapolis 500, the 24 Hours of Daytona, and the 24 Hours of Le Mans races. That is an incredible feat considering the two "24 Hours" races are especially grueling—they take place for a full day. These accomplishments made Foyt one of the greatest race drivers of all time.

FUN FACT

In the 24 Hours of Le Mans race, the person who drives the greatest number of laps in 24 hours is the winner.

DRIVER STATS

- **Years Raced**: 1963 to 1994
- **Wins**: 7
- **Awards**: 1972 Daytona 500 champion; named one of NASCAR's 75 Greatest Drivers; NASCAR Hall of Fame nominee

A. J. Foyt at the 1986 Daytona 500

JEFF GORDON

Jeff Gordon was named Rookie of the Year in 1991 when he joined NASCAR. It was the first of many successes. In 1992, he made his Winston Cup debut. It was his first major NASCAR race and the last race for another NASCAR legend: Richard Petty. In 1995, Gordon became the youngest NASCAR driver in modern racing to win

DRIVER STATS

- **Years Raced**: 1992 to 2016
- **Wins**: 93
- **Awards**: Rookie of the Year, 1993; Winner of four NASCAR championships; NASCAR Hall of Fame, inducted 2019

Jeff Gordon's racing team was known as the "Rainbow Warriors," named for his colorful number 24 Chevrolet.

Jeff Gordon celebrates a win at Kansas Speedway.

a Cup championship. He was only 24 years old. He went on to win championships in 1997, 1998, and 2001. He ranks third on NASCAR's all-time wins list.

NASCAR IN THE KNOW

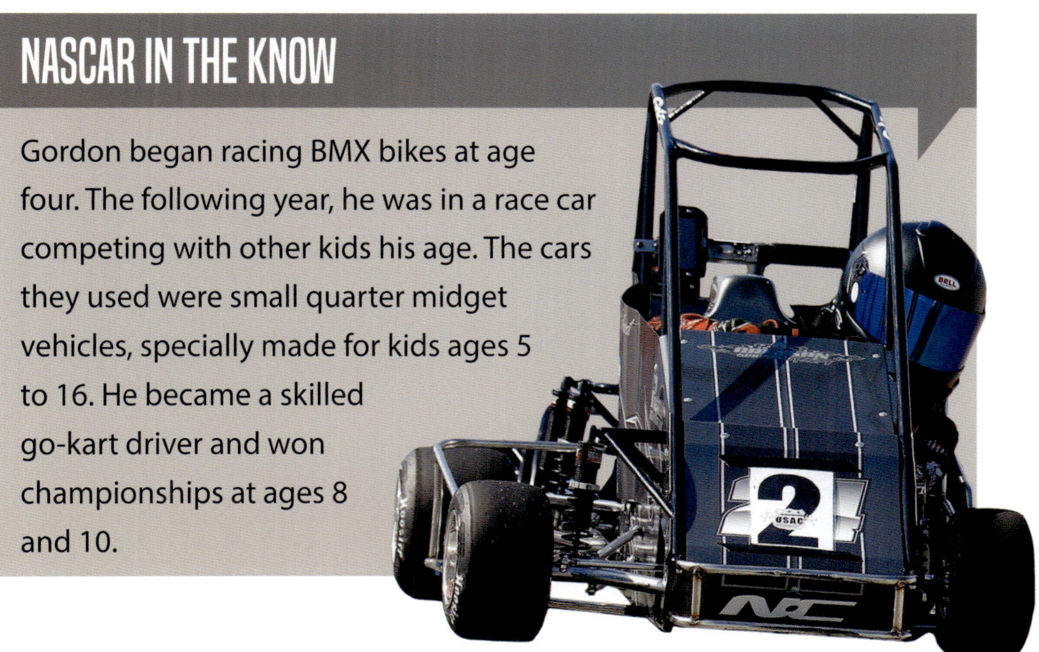

Gordon began racing BMX bikes at age four. The following year, he was in a race car competing with other kids his age. The cars they used were small quarter midget vehicles, specially made for kids ages 5 to 16. He became a skilled go-kart driver and won championships at ages 8 and 10.

HARRY GANT

In 1964, Harry Gant raced on a dirt track for the first time as a hobby. The following year, he won the track's championship. By 1967, his local track was paved. Gant started winning more races. He made his Cup debut in 1973 but didn't win a victory in a Cup race until 1982, becoming the oldest driver, at age 42, ever to win a Cup race. In 1992, Gant broke another record. At age 52, he became the oldest driver ever to win a NASCAR Winston Cup.

Harry Gant at the 1986 Daytona 500

DRIVER STATS

- **Years Raced**: 1973 to 1996
- **Wins**: 18
- **Awards**: Named one of NASCAR's 50 Greatest Drivers; Motorsports Hall of Fame, inducted 2006

DENNY HAMLIN

Denny Hamlin joined the Joe Gibbs racing team in 2006, and he has stayed with the team since. The same year, he became the first Rookie of the Year ever to qualify for the playoffs. Four years later, he won eight races and was runner-up for NASCAR's championship title. In 2015, he won NASCAR's All-Star race, and the $1 million prize that went with it. Hamlin has won first place at 16 of NASCAR's 24 tracks.

FUN FACT

NASCAR cars have removable steering wheels to make it easier for the drivers to get into and out of the cars.

DRIVER STATS

- **Years Raced**: 2006 to present
- **Wins**: 51 as of 2023
- **Awards**: Three-time Daytona 500 winner; three-time Southern 500 winner; named one of NASCAR's 75 Greatest Drivers

Denny Hamlin gets ready for a race at Auto Club Speedway.

KEVIN HARVICK

Kevin Harvick started racing stock cars in 1992 at age 17. By 1995, Harvick was racing in NASCAR's Truck Series. He made his Xfinity Series debut in 2000 and won the championship in 2001. The same year, Harvick took over Dale Earnhardt Sr.'s car after he died. By 2014, Harvick won his first Cup Series championship. He continues to be one of NASCAR's top drivers.

FUN FACT

In 2007, Kevin Harvick earned a stunning victory. He won the Daytona 500 after starting the race in 34th place!

DRIVER STATS

- **Years Raced**: 1995 to present
- **Wins**: 60 as of 2023
- **Awards**: Winner of one NASCAR championship, 2014; Named one of NASCAR's 75 Greatest Drivers

Kevin Harvick at Phoenix International Raceway

Bobby Isaac in the late 1950s

BOBBY ISAAC

Bobby Isaac was fascinated with racing at a young age. He began driving race cars on dirt tracks around his home state of North Carolina. By 1961, Isaac made his way up to NASCAR. It took him seven more years to really make his mark. In 1968, he won three races, then 17 races the following year, and in 1970, he took the championship.

DRIVER STATS

- **Years Raced**: 1961 to 1976
- **Wins**: 37
- **Awards**: Winner of one NASCAR championship; named one of NASCAR's 50 Greatest Drivers; NASCAR Hall of Fame, inducted 2016

DALE JARRETT

Dale Jarrett, his brother Glenn, and his father Ned were all race car drivers. Dale and his father are one of only two father-son NASCAR drivers who have both won championships. During his career, Dale won one NASCAR Cup Series championship and finished in the top five in six others. He also won the Daytona 500 three times.

Dale Jarrett in 1997

FUN FACT

Dale Jarrett won his first Daytona in 1993, barely beating Dale Earnhardt Sr.

DRIVER STATS

- **Years Raced**: 1984 to 2008
- **Wins**: 32
- **Awards**: Winner of one NASCAR championship; NASCAR Hall of Fame, inducted 2014

Ned Jarrett in 1965

NED JARRETT

Ned Jarrett spent 13 years racing for NASCAR in the early years of the sport. Between 1964 and 1965, he won 28 races. One of those races was the Southern 500 at the Darlington Speedway, one of NASCAR's most difficult tracks. During the race, Jarrett was so far in the lead, he won by 14 laps. That's a total distance of 17.5 miles (28.2 km). It is still the largest margin of victory of any NASCAR Cup race.

NASCAR IN THE KNOW

After retiring from NASCAR, Ned Jarrett became a sports television broadcaster. During his son Dale's first Daytona 500 race, the elder Jarrett was in the commentator's booth giving a play-by-play of the race his son would soon win.

DRIVER STATS

- **Years Raced**: 1953 to 1966
- **Wins**: 50
- **Awards**: Winner of two NASCAR championships; NASCAR Hall of Fame, inducted 2011

JIMMIE JOHNSON

DRIVER STATS

- **Years Raced**: 2001 to 2023
- **Wins**: 83
- **Awards**: Winner of seven NASCAR championships; named one of NASCAR's 75 Greatest Drivers; NASCAR Hall of Fame, inducted 2024

Jimmie Johnson's parents were both drivers of a different kind: his father operated bulldozers, and his mother was a school bus driver. Johnson had a passion to be behind the wheel too. He started racing motor bikes and race cars as a kid and showed natural talent. As a professional driver, he began to break records early in his career. He won the NASCAR championship five years in a row, from 2006 to 2010. With a total of seven championship wins, Johnson is tied with famed NASCAR drivers Richard Petty and Dale Earnhardt Sr. for the most series championships in history.

Jimmie Johnson celebrates a win at Charlotte Motor Speedway in 2012.

JUNIOR JOHNSON

Junior Johnson was not only a star driver, but he was also a successful NASCAR team owner. His biggest contribution to racing, however, came in the form of a new discovery. In 1960, Johnson was practicing at Daytona when he discovered a new technique, called drafting, to help increase speed. Johnson used drafting to win the 1960 Daytona 500.

Junior Johnson in 1960

DRIVER STATS

- **Years Raced**: 1955 to 1966
- **Wins**: 50
- **Awards**: Winner of six NASCAR championships (as an owner); named one of NASCAR's 50 Greatest Drivers; NASCAR Hall of Fame, inducted 2010

NASCAR IN THE KNOW

In drafting, one race car lines up directly behind another. The lead car blocks the movement of air, helping the car behind move forward. Drafting also helps the lead car, because the trailing car reduces the lead car's drag. As a result, both cars can go faster.

Matt Kenseth at Pocono Raceway

MATT KENSETH

There are only 12 NASCAR drivers that have won the Daytona 500 more than once, and Matt Kenseth is one of them, with two wins. Over 18 full-time seasons in NASCAR, Kenseth has won trophy after trophy in every race in the Cup Series.

For many years, Kenseth's car and his team's fire suits were bright yellow and black, the colors of their sponsor, DeWalt Tools. The team was nicknamed the "Killer Bees."

DRIVER STATS

- **Years Raced**: 1998 to 2020
- **Wins**: 39
- **Awards**: Rookie of the Year, 2000; winner of one Cup Series championship, 2003; winner of two Daytona 500 races; named one of NASCAR's 75 Greatest Drivers; NASCAR Hall of Fame, inducted 2023

Alan Kulwicki after winning the 1992 NASCAR Winston Cup Series

ALAN KULWICKI

Alan Kulwicki knew a lot about cars. Before he became a NASCAR driver, he was a mechanical engineer—he designed machines such as car engines. He joined NASCAR in 1986, and by 1992, he won his first championship. It was a surprising win because Kulwicki was 278 points behind!

Kulwicki's career was cut short. He only raced for nine seasons until his death in 1993. His legacy, however, lives on, and he's considered one of NASCAR's greatest drivers.

DRIVER STATS

- **Years Raced**: 1985 to 1993
- **Wins**: 5
- **Awards**: Winner of one Cup Series championship, 1992; named one of NASCAR's 50 Greatest Drivers; NASCAR Hall of Fame, inducted 2019

FUN FACT

The most points a driver can earn in a race is 60.

BOBBY LABONTE

Bobby Labonte grew up with a father and brother who also raced. Labonte finally became a full-time NASCAR Cup driver in 1993. He was the first driver to win championships in the Cup and Xfinity Series. Only three other drivers have matched this achievement.

Bobby Labonte

DRIVER STATS

- **Years Raced**: 1991; 1993 to 2016
- **Wins**: 21
- **Awards**: Winner of one Cup Series championship, 2000; named one of NASCAR's 75 Greatest Drivers; NASCAR Hall of Fame, inducted 2020

FUN FACT

Bobby and Terry Labonte are one of only two pairs of brothers who have both won Cup Series championships. Kurt and Kyle Busch are the other pair.

TERRY LABONTE

Terry Labonte had two nicknames during his NASCAR career. First, he was known as the "Iceman." He was known for always being cool under pressure. After a few years of racing with NASCAR under his belt, Labonte became known as the "Ironman" due to the more than 650 consecutive races in which he competed. Labonte holds the record for most time between series championship wins: 12 years.

DRIVER STATS

- **Years Raced**: 1978 to 2014
- **Wins**: 22
- **Awards**: Winner of two Cup Series championships, 1986 and 1996; named one of NASCAR's 50 Greatest Drivers; NASCAR Hall of Fame, inducted 2016

Terry Labonte

FRED LORENZEN

Fred Lorenzen was one of NASCAR's earlier drivers, and he was very popular with fans. During his best season in 1963, he finished in third place overall. This was quite a feat for Lorenzen because he only raced in 29 of the 55 races. Two years later, he won the coveted Daytona 500 trophy.

Fred Lorenzen was known as "Fearless Freddie" for his full-force style of racing.

FUN FACT

Fred Lorenzen was the first NASCAR driver to earn $100,000 in one year.

DRIVER STATS

- **Years Raced**: 1956 to 1972
- **Wins**: 26
- **Awards**: Winner of the 1965 Daytona 500; named one of NASCAR's 50 Greatest Drivers; NASCAR Hall of Fame, inducted 2015

DEWAYNE LOUIS "TINY" LUND

Though DeWayne Louis Lund's nickname was "Tiny," he was actually a towering 6 feet, 5 inches (2 m) tall. He joined NASCAR in the mid-1950s. In 1963, at the Daytona 500, Lund pulled another driver out of a burning car after an accident, saving his life. The driver, Marvin Panch, had to drop out of the Daytona 500 due to his injuries but suggested Lund take his place. Lund won the race.

DRIVER STATS

- **Years Raced**: 1955 to 1975
- **Wins**: 49
- **Awards**: Three-time Grand American champion; 1963 Daytona 500 champion; named one of NASCAR's 50 Greatest Drivers

FUN FACT

Tiny Lund had a passion for fishing. When he wasn't racing, he operated a fishing camp.

Tiny Lund

STERLING MARLIN

As a teenager, Sterling Marlin was an avid athlete. When not playing sports, he was helping his dad fix cars. His dad was a NASCAR driver, and Marlin knew he wanted to be one too. He made his NASCAR debut in 1976. He won the Daytona 500 two years in a row, in 1994 and 1995. Only two other drivers have done the same: Richard Petty and Cale Yarborough.

Sterling Marlin's NASCAR career spanned 33 years.

DRIVER STATS

- **Years Raced**: 1983 to 2010
- **Wins**: 10
- **Awards**: Rookie of the Year, 1983; named one of NASCAR's 75 Greatest Drivers, 2023

MARK MARTIN

Mark Martin's father owned a trucking company and sponsored small racing teams in the area around their hometown of Batesville, Arkansas. In 1973, at age 14, Martin asked his father to build him a race car. The following year, he drove it in his first stock car race and finished as the season winner of the Arkansas State Championship. During his NASCAR career, Martin had 395 top-ten finishes in the Cup Series, including multiple number-one spots. He also raced in every NASCAR series. With 49 wins, Martin is the record holder for most wins in NASCAR's Busch Series (now called the Xfinity Series).

FUN FACT

Mark Martin holds the record for the fastest 500-mile (805-km) race, completing the Winston 500 in just over 2 hours and 39 minutes.

DRIVER STATS

- **Years Raced**: 1981 to 2013
- **Wins**: 40
- **Awards**: Named one of NASCAR's 50 Greatest Drivers, 1998; NASCAR Hall of Fame, inducted 2017

Mark Martin at Pocono Raceway

Ryan Newman greets fans at Phoenix International Raceway.

RYAN NEWMAN

Ryan Newman is nicknamed "Rocket Man." He is not only fast on the track, but he also has a degree in engineering. At age 16, Newman became the first driver to win all three of the racing divisions of the United States Auto Club (USAC). Two years later, in 1995, he accomplished this feat for a second time. In 2000, Newman made his NASCAR Cup debut. Throughout his career, he's had multiple wins at every level of NASCAR.

DRIVER STATS

- **Years Raced**: 2002 to present
- **Wins**: 18
- **Awards**: Rookie of the Year, 2002; Driver of the Year, 2003; named one of NASCAR's 75 Greatest Drivers, 2023

Cotton Owens

COTTON OWENS

Cotton Owens had success as a NASCAR driver and even more as a team owner. After his successful driving career, Owens decided to build powerful race cars. One such car was a Dodge. It won 27 races with fellow racer David Pearson behind the wheel. Owens and Pearson made a racing dream team. Together, they won the 1966 NASCAR championship. Pearson continued to win many other races in cars that Owens built. The number 6 Dodge is on display at the NASCAR Hall of Fame.

DRIVER STATS

- **Years Raced**: 1950 to 1964
- **Wins**: 9 (38 as an owner)
- **Awards**: Named one of NASCAR's 50 Greatest Drivers; NASCAR Hall of Fame, inducted 2013

MARVIN PANCH

Before driving for NASCAR, Marvin Panch had been a successful racer in California. He was so good, founder Bill France Sr. and legendary driver Lee Petty asked Panch to drive for NASCAR. He began in 1951 and showcased his talent from the start. However, one of the biggest moments in Panch's NASCAR career was also one of the scariest. In 1963, he was in a fiery car crash at the Daytona Speedway. Fellow driver Tiny Lund pulled Panch out of the car, saving his life.

Marvin Panch

DRIVER STATS

- **Years Raced**: 1951 to 1966
- **Wins**: 17
- **Awards**: Daytona 500 champion, 1961; named one of NASCAR's 50 Greatest Drivers; nominated for NASCAR's Hall of Fame

Benny Parsons

BENNY PARSONS

Benny Parsons finished in the top ten in more than half of his races. He was also one fast driver. During the qualification races for the 1982 Winston 500 at the Talladega Speedway, he reached a speed of 200.176 miles per hour (322.2 kmh). This made him the first NASCAR driver to qualify for a race at speeds of more than 200 miles per hour (322 kmh).

DRIVER STATS

- **Years Raced**: 1964 to 1988
- **Wins**: 21
- **Awards**: Winner of one series championship; named one of NASCAR's 50 Greatest Drivers; NASCAR Hall of Fame, inducted 2017

FUN FACT

Though NASCAR race cars move at speeds of up to 200 miles per hour (322 kmh), they don't have speedometers.

DANICA PATRICK

As one of the few women in professional motorsports, Danica Patrick broke barriers as well as records. Patrick's racing career started at age 10 when she began racing go-karts. In high school, with many national wins behind her, she moved to the United Kingdom to compete in European road racing.

In 2002, Patrick moved back to the United States and raced open-wheel race cars, qualifying for the Indianapolis 500. In 2005,

Danica Patrick holds the record for the most top-ten finishes of any female in the NASCAR Cup Series.

she became the first woman to lead in the Indianapolis 500. She finished fourth in the race.

In 2010, Patrick began driving for NASCAR's Nationwide Series, now the Xfinity Series. By 2011, she drove in both the Nationwide and Cup Series. Two years later, in 2013, she became the first woman to lead a lap at Daytona. She finished the race in eighth place, the highest position ever for a woman.

During the 2013 Daytona 500, Patrick became the first woman to win a NASCAR Cup Series pole. With the fastest car in the qualifying rounds, she had the best starting position for the race.

In 2018, Patrick ended her racing career by competing in what was called the "Danica Double"—the Daytona 500 and the Indianapolis 500.

NASCAR IN THE KNOW

In open-wheel racing, the wheels are on the outside of the car. These cars usually have just one seat, and the cockpit is open. The Indianapolis 500 is considered the most prestigious open-wheel race.

DRIVER STATS

- **Years Raced**: 2012 to 2018
- **Wins**: 0 (7 top tens)
- **Awards**: NASCAR Nationwide Series Most Popular Driver, 2012

David Pearson

DAVID PEARSON

In 1960, at age 26, David Pearson drove his first race at the Grand National, now the Cup Series. He was also named Rookie of the Year. His most successful racing years were 1966, 1968, and 1973, when he won a combined 42 races. In 1976, he won the coveted Daytona 500. Over his 27-year career, he earned more than 100 wins. The only person to have more wins is Richard Petty.

FUN FACT

David Pearson is known as the "Silver Fox" because of his smart approach to racing.

DRIVER STATS

- **Years Raced**: 1960 to 1986
- **Wins**: 105
- **Awards**: Rookie of the Year, 1960; winner of three NASCAR championships: 1966, 1968, 1969; NASCAR Hall of Fame, inducted 2011

LEE PETTY

Before becoming a race car driver, Lee Petty was a farmer. He also drove trucks and taxis and enjoyed repairing cars. In 1949, he heard that a new organization called NASCAR would be holding a race in Charlotte, North Carolina. He entered, driving his family's Buick. Petty was hooked. He started racing professionally, winning numerous NASCAR races and three championships, including the very first Daytona 500.

It took officials three days to call the 1959 Daytona 500 for Lee Petty. The finish between Petty and fellow driver Johnny Beauchamp was too close to call. Judges needed to wait to see the photo taken at the finish line. Back then, it took several days to get photos developed.

DRIVER STATS

- **Years Raced**: 1949 to 1964
- **Wins**: 54
- **Awards**: Winner of three NASCAR championships: 1954, 1958, and 1959; NASCAR Hall of Fame, inducted 2011

Lee Petty after his win of the 1959 Daytona 500

RICHARD PETTY

When Richard Petty got into racing, NASCAR was going from a little-known sport to the superspeedways. He would soon dominate the sport. He began in the Grand National Series (now the Cup Series) in 1958 with the encouragement of his father, Lee. That year, he earned Rookie of the Year. In 1960, he won his first Cup race, and seven years later, he broke the record for most first-places finishes, with 27 wins, including a Cup championship.

Richard Petty is known as "The King" of NASCAR.

DRIVER STATS

- **Years Raced**: 1958 to 1992
- **Wins**: 200
- **Awards**: Rookie of the Year, 1959; winner of seven NASCAR championships; NASCAR Hall of Fame, inducted 2010

NASCAR IN THE KNOW

Richard Petty raced in 1,185 NASCAR events and holds the NASCAR record for most wins with a staggering 200 victories. He is the most successful driver in the sport.

Glen "Fireball" Roberts

GLEN "FIREBALL" ROBERTS

Glen "Fireball" Roberts got his flashy nickname as a teenager. He could pitch a baseball with intense speed, like a fireball flying through the air. As a race car driver, Roberts was a star of the Daytona 500 International Speedway. He won the Firecracker 250, his first Daytona race, in 1959. It was also the same year the raceway opened. Six more Daytona wins followed. Roberts was intense behind the wheel and one of the first superstars in the sport.

DRIVER STATS

- **Years Raced**: 1950 to 1964
- **Wins**: 33
- **Awards**: 1962 Daytona 500 champion; named one of NASCAR's 50 Greatest Drivers; NASCAR Hall of Fame, inducted 2014

WENDELL SCOTT

Wendell Scott was the first Black driver and team owner to compete full-time in NASCAR's top series. Before racing cars, Scott served in World War II (1939 to 1945), where he mastered his mechanical skills working on military vehicles. He started racing in 1947, driving in more than 100 local races.

In 1961, Scott made his NASCAR debut in Spartanburg, South Carolina. He had a successful year with five top-five finishes. By 1963, he won his first NASCAR Premier Series race

Wendell Scott broke barriers as the first Black driver to win a NASCAR Cup Series race.

Wendell Scott traveled to races with his family. They served as his pit crew and helped Scott maintain his cars.

(now the Cup Series) and made history by becoming the first Black driver to win a race at NASCAR's highest level. But he was not declared the winner right away, though it was clear he had won. The win was given to fellow driver Buck Baker at first. Officials did not want to give the top award to a Black man.

Scott was declared the winner a few hours after the race ended, but he never received his trophy. Scott spent the next 13 years racing, earning top-ten finishes in more than 25 percent of all his races. He accomplished all of this despite death threats and discrimination. In 2015, Scott was inducted into the NASCAR Hall of Fame.

DRIVER STATS

- **Years Raced**: 1961 to 1973
- **Wins**: 1
- **Awards**: NASCAR Hall of Fame, inducted 2015

Ricky Rudd signs autographs at Pocono Raceway.

RICKY RUDD

Ricky Rudd started in 788 consecutive races during his career. That's one of the highest numbers of starts in NASCAR history. It earned Rudd the nickname "Ironman." Only Jeff Gordon has had more consecutive starts. Rudd continued to race until he was 50 years old, winning at least one race a year for 16 consecutive seasons. A few years after retiring, Rudd made his television debut when he appeared in the TV show *Dallas*. He played himself—a race car driver!

DRIVER STATS

- **Years Raced**: 1975 to 2007
- **Wins**: 23
- **Awards**: Cup Series Rookie of the Year, 1977; named one of NASCAR's 50 Greatest Drivers; NASCAR Hall of Fame nominee

TONY STEWART

Tony Stewart holds a very unique record: he drove IndyCar and NASCAR races on the same day, on two different occasions! As a young professional racer, Stewart raced for the United States Auto Club (USAC) and received a Triple Crown, winning all three of their major races. In 1999, Stewart joined NASCAR. Today, he co-owns Stewart-Haas Racing, a championship-winning team.

DRIVER STATS

- **Years Raced**: 1999 to 2016
- **Wins**: 49
- **Awards**: Rookie of the Year, 1999; winner of three NASCAR championships; NASCAR Hall of Fame, inducted 2020

FUN FACT

Tony Stewart is one of only two drivers to win a championship while being a driver and team owner.

Tony Stewart wins at Las Vegas Motor Speedway.

HERB THOMAS

Herb Thomas had many firsts in his career. He was one of NASCAR's early drivers and the first NASCAR driver to win two championships, in 1951 and in 1953. His many wins also made him the first true racing star in the United States.

Thomas became a three-time winner at the Darlington Raceway after winning the Southern 500 race in 1951, 1954, and 1955—another first!

DRIVER STATS

- **Years Raced**: 1949 to 1962
- **Wins**: 48
- **Awards**: Winner of two NASCAR championships; NASCAR Hall of Fame, inducted 2013

Herb Thomas

Curtis Turner

CURTIS TURNER

Curtis Turner earned a reputation as a great racer during his early racing years around his home state of Virginia. In 1949, he was invited to join NASCAR.

But 12 years later, he was banned for life from NASCAR. Owner Bill France Sr. was angered that Turner and fellow driver Tim Flock were trying to form a union. In 1965, France was moved to lift the ban after the deaths of Joe Weatherly and Fireball Roberts. After the tragic losses, France wanted to get familiar and popular drivers back on the track. Upon his return, Turner quickly began winning races again.

DRIVER STATS

- **Years Raced**: 1949 to 1968
- **Wins**: 17
- **Awards**: Named one of NASCAR's 50 Greatest Drivers; International Motorsports Hall of Fame; NASCAR Hall of Fame, inducted 2016

FUN FACT

In 1968, Curtis Turner became the first NASCAR driver to be on the cover of *Sports Illustrated* magazine.

DARRELL "BUBBA" WALLACE

In 2018, Darrell "Bubba" Wallace became the first full-time Black driver in NASCAR's premier Cup Series. In 2021, Wallace made history once again, becoming the first Black driver to win a NASCAR Cup Series race since Wendell Scott's victory in 1963.

In addition to racing for NASCAR, Wallace is a graduate of the Drive for Diversity program and has played an important role in helping to build NASCAR's diversity and equality.

FUN FACT

Bubba Wallace played an important role in helping to ban the Confederate Flag at NASCAR races.

Darrell "Bubba" Wallace

DRIVER STATS

- **Years Raced**: 2012 to present
- **Wins**: 2
- **Awards**: UARA-Stars (now ARCA) Series Rookie of the Year, 2008; K&N Pro Series East Rookie of the Year, 2010

Rusty Wallace

RUSTY WALLACE

Before coming to NASCAR, Rusty Wallace raced for the United States Auto Club (USAC) and won the USAC's Rookie of the Year. In 1983, he had another major win when he won the American Speed Association (ASA) championship. He started for NASCAR in 1980, and by 1984, he was a full-time Cup driver, winning NASCAR's Rookie of the Year. By 2000, Wallace had his 50th career win, becoming only the 10th driver in NASCAR history to reach that number. After retiring from racing, Wallace became a team owner and a NASCAR analyst on ESPN.

DRIVER STATS

- **Years Raced**: 1980 to 2005
- **Wins**: 55
- **Awards**: Rookie of the Year, 1984; winner of one NASCAR championship; NASCAR Hall of Fame, inducted 2013

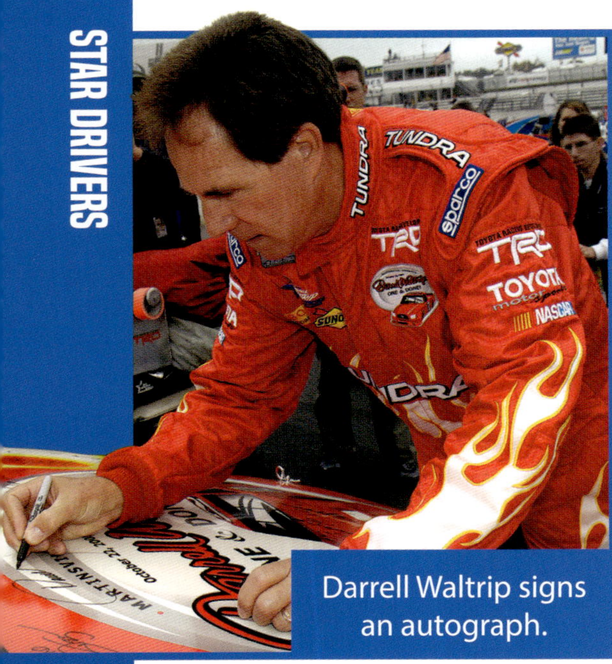

Darrell Waltrip signs an autograph.

DARRELL WALTRIP

Darrell Waltrip worked with his father to fix up an old Chevrolet to race on a dirt track close to his home in Kentucky. He was soon racing on the Kentucky Motor Speedway. Waltrip also began promoting races on television and radio. He was a natural on the air.

Waltrip began driving for NASCAR in 1972. His most successful years were from 1981 to 1986. In 1981 and 1982, he won 12 races each year. The only driver to win more races in a single season is Jeff Gordon, who won 13 races in 1998.

Waltrip's last win was in 1992. After retiring from NASCAR in 2000, Waltrip became a television sports broadcaster.

DRIVER STATS

- **Years Raced**: 1972 to 2000
- **Wins**: 84
- **Awards**: Most Popular Driver Award, 1989 and 1990; named one of NASCAR's 50 Greatest Drivers; winner of three NASCAR championships

FUN FACT

Darrell Waltrip drove in more than 800 races during his 29-year career.

Joe Weatherly (right) celebrates a win with car owner Bud Moore in 1961.

JOE WEATHERLY

Joe Weatherly was known as the "Clown Prince of Stock Car Racing" for his lively personality and incredible skill on the track. He was a two-time winner of the NASCAR Grand National Series (now known as the Cup Series). Before joining NASCAR's premier series, Weatherly raced for a now defunct NASCAR convertible series and won 12 races. Unfortunately, his life was cut short after an accident in the Motor Trend 500 race in 1964.

DRIVER STATS

- **Years Raced**: 1952 to 1964
- **Wins**: 25
- **Awards**: Named one of NASCAR's 50 Greatest Drivers; NASCAR Hall of Fame, inducted 2015

Rex White

REX WHITE

Before becoming a race car driver, NASCAR champion Rex White worked in a service station in Washington, DC. There, White kept seeing posters for races at Lanham Speedway in Maryland. He was interested in seeing a race, so he saved money for tickets and went with some family. White's life was changed. He joined NASCAR and did not look back.

DRIVER STATS

- **Years Raced**: 1956 to 1964
- **Wins**: 28
- **Awards**: Winner of one NASCAR Cup Series championship; named one of NASCAR's 50 Greatest Drivers; NASCAR Hall of Fame, inducted 2015

FUN FACT

Rex White's hometown of Spartanburg, South Carolina, is also home to four other NASCAR Hall of Fame drivers: David Pearson, Cale Yarborough, Cotton Owens, and Bud Moore.

GLEN WOOD

Glen Wood was a founding member of the Wood Brothers racing team, and he was also the team's driver. The team started for fun in 1950, but by 1954, it became a highly competitive racing team within NASCAR. Wood's star was also rising, and he won NASCAR's Most Popular Driver Award in 1959. After retiring from driving, Wood did not leave the track. Instead, he became a crew chief for some of NASCAR's top drivers.

DRIVER STATS

- **Years Raced**: 1953 to 1964
- **Wins**: 4
- **Awards**: Named one of NASCAR's 50 Greatest Drivers; NASCAR Hall of Fame, inducted 2012

Glen Wood

WILLIAM CALEB "CALE" YARBOROUGH

William Caleb "Cale" Yarborough began racing stock cars as a teenager, after attending a Southern 500 race at 12 years old. He made his NASCAR debut at 18 and spent the next 31 years racing.

One of his greatest accomplishments was winning the Grand National (now the Cup Series) three years in a row: 1976, 1977, and 1978. He was the first driver to win three consecutive series championships. During the 1977 Grand National race, Yarborough won the

Cale Yarborough

Cale Yarborough's Chevrolet Chevelle

championship by beating star driver Richard Petty. It was one of Yarborough's best racing years.

Yarborough ranks second overall after Petty for most miles led over his NASCAR career. He led 34,079.9 miles (54,846.3 km) over other drivers. He drove in 558 races and led in at least one lap in 340 of those races. Two years before retiring in 1988, Yarborough wrote an autobiography about his life and experience as a NASCAR driver.

DRIVER STATS

- **Years Raced**: 1957 to 1988
- **Wins**: 83
- **Awards**: Winner of three championships; named one of NASCAR's 50 Greatest Drivers, 1998; NASCAR Hall of Fame, inducted 2012

FUN FACT

One of Cale Yarborough's first jobs was working at the Holman-Moody racing shop in Charlotte, North Carolina. He was paid $1.25 per hour.

CUP SERIES DRIVERS

Cars race at the Charlotte Motor Speedway.

Cup Series drivers are the top drivers in NASCAR. Most began racing at a young age. Some have raced in completely different motorsports, such as motocross. Many began their NASCAR careers in other tiers of racing, such as the Xfinity Series or the Truck Series. But regardless of their start in the Cup Series, these drivers are at the top of the sport.

FUN FACT

Racing causes a driver's heartbeat to race, just like any other physical activity. Though drivers are sitting, they require a lot of endurance to race.

A. J. Allmendinger

A. J. ALLMENDINGER

A. J. Allmendinger's nickname is "The Dinger." Besides racing cars, he also is a sports broadcaster on television.

DRIVER STATS

- **Hometown**: Los Gatos, California
- **Date of Birth**: December 16, 1981
- **Team**: Kaulig Racing
- **Car Model**: Chevrolet Camaro ZL1
- **Car Number**: 16

Aric Almirola

ARIC ALMIROLA

Aric Almirola began racing go-karts at age eight. He now drives full-time for NASCAR, driving Richard Petty's number 43 Ford.

DRIVER STATS

- **Hometown**: Tampa, Florida
- **Date of Birth**: March 14, 1984
- **Team**: Stewart-Haas Racing
- **Car Model**: Ford Mustang GT
- **Car Number**: 10

Christopher Bell

CHRISTOPHER BELL

Christopher Bell started racing in junior leagues as a child. By age 19, he was racing open-wheel cars known as sprint cars. He began racing in NASCAR in 2015.

DRIVER STATS

- **Hometown**: Norman, Oklahoma
- **Date of Birth**: December 16, 1994
- **Team**: Joe Gibbs Racing
- **Car Model**: Toyota Camry
- **Car Number**: 20

RYAN BLANEY

Ryan Blaney's first Cup Series win was at Pocono Raceway in 2017. His ninth win was at Talladega Superspeedway in 2023.

DRIVER STATS

- **Hometown**: Hartford, Ohio
- **Date of Birth**: December 31, 1993
- **Team**: Team Penske
- **Car Model**: Ford Mustang GT
- **Car Number**: 12

Ryan Blaney

Alex Bowman

DRIVER STATS

- **Hometown**: Tucson, Arizona
- **Date of Birth**: April 25, 1993
- **Team**: Hendrick Motorsports
- **Car Model**: Chevrolet Camaro ZL1
- **Car Number**: 48

ALEX BOWMAN

Alex Bowman was the ARCA Menards Series Rookie of the Year in 2012, the same year he began racing in NASCAR. He started in the Cup Series full-time in 2017, taking over as driver of Dale Earnhardt Jr.'s number 88 Chevrolet after his retirement. In 2021, Bowman began driving the number 48 Chevrolet. He finished fifth place in the 2023 Daytona 500.

CHASE BRISCOE

Chase Briscoe made his NASCAR debut driving for the Truck Series in 2017. By 2018, he was racing the Xfinity Series. After winning an impressive nine Xfinity races in 2020, he moved up to NASCAR's Cup Series for the 2021 season and continues to have success there.

DRIVER STATS

- **Hometown**: Mitchell, Indiana
- **Date of Birth**: December 15, 1994
- **Team**: Stewart-Haas Racing
- **Car Model**: Ford Mustang GT
- **Car Number**: 14

Chase Briscoe

CHRIS BUESCHER

In 2011, Chris Buescher was the ARCA Series Rookie of the Year and became the youngest champion in the history of the series at 19 years old. Buescher soon moved into NASCAR's Xfinity Series, and by 2016, he made his Cup Series debut.

DRIVER STATS

- **Hometown**: Prosper, Texas
- **Date of Birth**: October 29, 1992
- **Team**: RFK Racing
- **Car Model**: Ford Mustang GT
- **Car Number**: 17

FUN FACT

Chris Buescher started racing at age six, competing in motocross, a type of motorcycle racing.

HARRISON BURTON

Harrison Burton has been racing since he was just a kid. At age 15, he became the youngest driver to compete in the NASCAR ARCA Series. He moved up through the Xfinity and Truck Series, and in 2022, he joined the Cup Series.

Harrison Burton

DRIVER STATS

- **Hometown**: Huntersville, North Carolina
- **Date of Birth**: October 9, 2000
- **Team**: Wood Brothers Racing
- **Car Model**: Ford Mustang GT
- **Car Number**: 21

KYLE BUSCH

Kyle Busch

Kyle Busch has been racing for NASCAR for almost 20 years. He is one of the organization's most decorated drivers. In his Cup Series career, he has competed in more than 640 races and has already been named one of NASCAR's 75 Greatest Drivers. Busch holds the record for most NASCAR wins over all three series: Cup, Xfinity, and Truck.

DRIVER STATS

- **Hometown**: Las Vegas, Nevada
- **Date of Birth**: May 2, 1985
- **Team**: Richard Childress Racing
- **Car Model**: Chevrolet Camaro ZL1
- **Car Number**: 8

FUN FACT

Kyle Busch's team has been sponsored by M&Ms candy.

WILLIAM BYRON

William Byron began racing in the Truck Series in 2015 and in the Xfinity Series in 2016. He won the championship that same year. In 2018, Byron moved up to the Cup Series and was named the Cup Series Rookie of the Year.

DRIVER STATS

- **Hometown**: Charlotte, North Carolina
- **Date of Birth**: November 29, 1997
- **Team**: Hendrick Motorsports
- **Car Model**: Chevrolet Camaro ZL1
- **Car Number**: 24

ROSS CHASTAIN

Ross Chastain grew up on his family's watermelon farm. As a child, he got into racing short tracks. Chastain began racing in NASCAR in 2011. In 2019, he joined the Cup Series. Today, he races for all three of NASCAR's racing series.

Ross Chastain

DRIVER STATS

- **Hometown**: Alva, Florida
- **Date of Birth**: December 4, 1992
- **Team**: Truckhouse Racing Team
- **Car Model**: Chevrolet Camaro ZL1
- **Car Number**: 1

AUSTIN CINDRIC

Austin Cindric started competing in go-karting before moving to the world of NASCAR. By 2017, he was racing in the Truck Series and Xfinity Series. His career highlights include winning the NASCAR Xfinity Series championship in 2020 and the Daytona 500 in 2022.

Austin Cindric

DRIVER STATS

- **Hometown**: Mooresville, North Carolina
- **Date of Birth**: September 2, 1998
- **Team**: Team Penske
- **Car Model**: Ford Mustang GT
- **Car Number**: 2

AUSTIN DILLON

Austin Dillon is the grandson of legendary team owner Richard Childress and spent his childhood surrounded by race cars. In 2009, he began racing in NASCAR. In 2018, he won the Daytona 500.

DRIVER STATS

- **Hometown**: Welcome, North Carolina
- **Date of Birth**: April 27, 1990
- **Team**: Richard Childress Racing
- **Car Model**: Chevrolet Camaro ZL1
- **Car Number**: 3

Austin Dillon

TY DILLON

Ty Dillon is the younger brother of racer Austin Dillion. Like his brother, he grew up around racing. His journey started with racing go-karts, then cars in the ARCA series. He made his NASCAR debut in 2011, and in 2014, he joined the Cup Series.

DRIVER STATS

- **Hometown**: Welcome, North Carolina
- **Date of Birth**: February 27, 1992
- **Team**: Spire Motorsports
- **Car Model**: Chevrolet Camaro ZL1
- **Car Number**: 77

CHASE ELLIOTT

Chase Elliott grew up as the son of NASCAR Hall of Famer Bill Elliott. Chase climbed through the ranks of racing, making it to NASCAR's Xfinity Series at only 18 years old. He became the youngest NASCAR Xfinity Series champion. In 2020, he secured his first NASCAR Cup Series championship. At age 27, Elliott was already named one of NASCAR's Greatest Drivers.

Chase Elliott

DRIVER STATS

- **Hometown**: Dawsonville, Georgia
- **Date of Birth**: November 28, 1995
- **Team**: Hendrick Motorsports
- **Car Model**: Chevrolet Camaro ZL1
- **Car Number**: 9

TY GIBBS

Ty Gibbs got his passion for racing from his grandfather, legendary team owner Joe Gibbs. Before joining NASCAR's Xfinity Series, he drove for ARCA, winning a championship in 2021. In 2022, Gibbs won seven races in the Xfinity Series, winning another championship. By 2023, Gibbs was racing full-time in the Cup Series.

DRIVER STATS

- **Hometown**: Charlotte, North Carolina
- **Date of Birth**: October 4, 2002
- **Team**: Joe Gibbs Racing
- **Car Model**: Toyota Camry
- **Car Number**: 54

TODD GILLILAND

In 2015, Todd Gilliland became the youngest racer in the ARCA Series, where he won two championships in a row. Gilliland was only 15 years old. He worked his way through the NASCAR Series, and in 2022, he began racing in the Cup Series. He made his debut at the Daytona 500 that same year.

DRIVER STATS

- **Hometown**: Statesville, North Carolina
- **Date of Birth**: May 15, 2000
- **Team**: Front Row Motorsports
- **Car Model**: Ford Mustang GT
- **Car Number**: 38

JUSTIN HALEY

Justin Haley began racing in NASCAR's Truck Series at age 16 in 2015. He moved up to the Xfinity Series in 2018 and drove his first Cup Series race in 2019.

DRIVER STATS

- **Hometown**: Winamac, Indiana
- **Date of Birth**: April 28, 1999
- **Team**: Kaulig Racing
- **Car Model**: Chevrolet Camaro ZL1
- **Car Number**: 31

Justin Haley

ERIK JONES

At age 14, Erik Jones was the youngest winner in a major race for the American Speed Association (ASA). He began racing in the Truck Series and, later, in the Xfinity Series. At age 19, he made his Cup Series debut. In 2017, he was the Cup Series Rookie of the Year.

Erik Jones

DRIVER STATS

- **Hometown**: Byron, Michigan
- **Date of Birth**: May 30, 1996
- **Team**: Legacy Motor Club
- **Car Model**: Chevrolet Camaro ZL1
- **Car Number**: 43

BRAD KESELOWSKI

As a teen, Brad Keselowski worked in his father's racing shop. In 2000, at age 16, he started racing stock cars, and just four years later, he was racing for NASCAR's Truck Series. He made his way up to the Cup Series in 2008.

FUN FACT

All NASCAR drivers must weigh 200 pounds (90.7 kg) in order to race. This includes their helmet. Weights are added to the car if a driver does not meet this requirement.

DRIVER STATS

- **Hometown**: Rochester, Michigan
- **Date of Birth**: February 12, 1984
- **Team**: RFK Racing
- **Car Model**: Ford Mustang GT
- **Car Number**: 6

COREY LAJOIE

Corey Lajoie grew up watching his father, Randy Lajoie, race all across the country and win championships. Corey started his racing career in what is now the ARCA Series, and by 2013, he had earned multiple victories. In 2014, he began racing in the Cup Series where he has had multiple top-ten finishes.

Corey Lajoie

DRIVER STATS

- **Hometown**: Concord, North Carolina
- **Date of Birth**: September 25, 1991
- **Team**: Spire Motorsports
- **Car Model**: Chevrolet Camaro ZL1
- **Car Number**: 7

KYLE LARSON

Kyle Larson made his NASCAR debut in 2012, winning two races early on. Larson moved up to the Cup Series in 2014, debuting at the Daytona 500. In 2021, he led in more than 2,500 laps in Cup Series races, the second highest number in history.

Kyle Larson

DRIVER STATS

- **Hometown**: Elk Grove, California
- **Date of Birth**: July 31, 1992
- **Team**: Hendrick Motorsports
- **Car Model**: Chevrolet Camaro ZL1
- **Car Number**: 5

JOEY LOGANO

In 2008, Joey Logano made his Xfinity debut at age 18. He drove his first race in the Cup Series that same year. He's now a two-time Cup Series champion.

Joey Logano

DRIVER STATS

- **Hometown**: Middletown, Connecticut
- **Date of Birth**: May 24, 1990
- **Team**: Team Penske
- **Car Model**: Ford Mustang GT
- **Car Number**: 22

MICHAEL MCDOWELL

Michael McDowell's racing journey goes back to his childhood in the 1980s when he raced bicycles. In 2007, McDowell started racing stock cars. He has earned four ARCA Series wins and was named Rookie of the Year. He also started racing in the NASCAR Xfinity and Truck Series. In 2008, he joined NASCAR's Cup Series, where he has multiple wins and more than 30 top-ten finishes.

DRIVER STATS

- **Hometown**: Glendale, Arizona
- **Date of Birth**: December 21, 1984
- **Team**: Front Row Motorsports
- **Car Model**: Ford Mustang GT
- **Car Number**: 34

Michael McDowell

B. J. MCLEOD

B. J. McLeod has been racing nearly his whole life, beginning with ATVs at age three. In 2010, he made his NASCAR Truck Series debut. He soon started racing in the Xfinity Series and made his Cup Series debut in 2015. He drove the Daytona 500 for the first time in 2019. In addition to being a driver, McLeod is also a team owner with cars competing in the Xfinity and Truck Series.

DRIVER STATS

- **Hometown**: Wauchula, Florida
- **Date of Birth**: November 17, 1983
- **Team**: Live Fast Motorsports
- **Car Model**: Chevrolet Camaro ZL1
- **Car Number**: 78

RYAN PREECE

Ryan Preece began his NASCAR career in the Whelen Series racing open-wheel cars. In 2013, he joined the Xfinity Series, and in 2015, he raced for the first time in the Cup Series.

DRIVER STATS

- **Hometown**: Berlin, Connecticut
- **Date of Birth**: October 25, 1990
- **Team**: Stewart-Haas Racing
- **Car Model**: Ford Mustang GT
- **Car Number**: 41

Ryan Preece

TYLER REDDICK

Tyler Reddick began racing in NASCAR's Truck Series at age 17. By 2019, he made his Cup Series debut at the Daytona 500. He has had more than 50 top-ten finishes and five wins.

DRIVER STATS

- **Hometown**: Corning, California
- **Date of Birth**: January 11, 1996
- **Team**: 23XI Racing
- **Car Model**: Toyota Camry
- **Car Number**: 45

RICKY STENHOUSE JR.

Ricky Stenhouse Jr. developed a love for racing while watching his dad race sprint cars. In 2008, he was racing in NASCAR's ARCA Racing Series, and in 2009, he joined the Xfinity Series. In 2013, he started racing for the Cup Series and was named Rookie of the Year. He's since racked up more than 50 top-ten finishes.

DRIVER STATS

- **Hometown**: Olive Branch, Mississippi
- **Date of Birth**: October 2, 1987
- **Team**: JTG Daugherty Racing
- **Car Model**: Chevrolet Camaro ZL1
- **Car Number**: 47

Ricky Stenhouse Jr.

Daniel Suárez

DANIEL SUÁREZ

Daniel Suárez's journey to NASCAR started from his early days in Mexico where he raced go-karts. In 2008, he started mini-stock racing in NASCAR Mexico, winning the Rookie of the Year award in 2010. Suárez made his NASCAR debut in the United States in 2011. In 2016, he won the Xfinity Series championship, making history as the first Mexican-born driver to win a NASCAR national series race. Suárez has since joined the Cup Series.

DRIVER STATS

- **Hometown**: Monterrey, Mexico
- **Date of Birth**: January 7, 1992
- **Team**: Trackhouse Racing Team
- **Car Model**: Chevrolet Camaro ZL1
- **Car Number**: 99

MARTIN TRUEX JR.

As the son of a race car driver, Martin Truex Jr. grew up around stock car racing. In 2001, Truex Jr. made his NASCAR debut in the Xfinity Series, driving for his father's team. Truex Jr. began racing in the Cup Series full-time in 2003. He has since raced in more than 640 races and has had more than 275 top tens and more than 30 wins.

DRIVER STATS

- **Hometown**: Mayetta, New Jersey
- **Date of Birth**: June 29, 1980
- **Team**: Joe Gibbs Racing
- **Car Model**: Toyota Camry
- **Car Number**: 19

ANTHONY ALFREDO

Anthony Alfredo joined NASCAR in 2019. He started in the Truck Series, and by 2020, he made his way up to the Xfinity Series. In 2021, Alfredo drove in the Cup Series, competing in more than 35 races. In 2023, Alfredo went back to the Xfinity Series, where he continues to race.

DRIVER STATS

- **Hometown**: Ridgefield, Connecticut
- **Date of Birth**: March 31, 1999
- **Team Name**: B. J. McLeod Motorsports
- **Car Model**: Chevrolet Camaro SS
- **Car Number**: 78

Justin Allgaier

JUSTIN ALLGAIER

Justin Allgaier competes full-time in the Xfinity Series, but he has competed in the Cup Series as well. In 2018, he was the Xfinity Series regular season champion. He has had more than 20 wins and almost 250 top tens.

DRIVER STATS

- **Hometown**: Riverton, Illinois
- **Date of Birth**: June 6, 1986
- **Team Name**: JR Motorsports
- **Car Model**: Chevrolet Camaro SS
- **Car Number**: 7

Josh Berry

JOSH BERRY

Josh Berry's racing career began in go-karting. In 2011, he earned a Late Model Most Popular Driver title. In 2012, Berry won another championship in NASCAR's Late Model Series, a special race with the latest model cars. By 2014, Josh was racing in the Xfinity Series. He has also spent time racing in the Truck and Cup Series.

DRIVER STATS

- **Hometown**: Hendersonville, Tennessee
- **Date of Birth**: October 22, 1990
- **Team Name**: Stewart-Haas Racing
- **Car Model**: Ford Mustang
- **Car Number**: 4

Jeremy Clements

JEREMY CLEMENTS

Jeremy Clements's grandfather, Crawford Clements, was a successful NASCAR team owner and engine builder, and Jeremy's uncle, Louis Clements, was a Crew Chief. In 2003, Clements made his Xfinity Series debut.

DRIVER STATS

- **Hometown**: Spartanburg, South Carolina
- **Date of Birth**: January 16, 1985
- **Team Name**: Jeremy Clements Racing
- **Car Model**: Chevrolet Camaro SS
- **Car Number**: 51

COLE CUSTER

Cole Custer began racing in the Truck Series at age 16. At age 19, in 2017, he moved up to the Xfinity Series. In 2020, he was named Rookie of the Year for the Cup Series.

DRIVER STATS

- **Hometown**: Ladera Ranch, California
- **Date of Birth**: January 23, 1998
- **Team Name**: Stewart-Haas Racing
- **Car Model**: Ford Mustang GT
- **Car Number**: 00

JEFFREY EARNHARDT

Jeffrey Earnhardt comes from a legendary NASCAR family. He is the grandson of seven-time NASCAR Cup champion Dale Earnhardt Sr. and the nephew of Dale Earnhardt Jr. Jeffrey began racing in the Truck Series in 2011. By 2014, he was racing full-time in the Xfinity Series. He has also raced in the Cup Series.

DRIVER STATS

- **Hometown**: Mooresville, North Carolina
- **Date of Birth**: June 22, 1989
- **Team Name**: Alpha Prime Racing
- **Car Model**: Chevrolet Camaro SS
- **Car Number**: 44

Jeffrey Earnhardt

JOEY GASE

In 2011, Joey Gase began competing in the Xfinity Series. By 2014, he made his Cup Series debut and drove in the series for multiple years. He currently drives in both the Xfinity and Cup Series and has driven in more than 350 races between the two competitions.

DRIVER STATS

- **Hometown**: Cedar Rapids, Iowa
- **Date of Birth**: February 8, 1993
- **Team Name**: Emerling-Gase Motorsports
- **Car Model**: Ford Mustang GT
- **Car Number**: 53

Gray Gaulding

GRAY GAULDING

In 2013, Gray Gaulding raced his first season with NASCAR's ARCA Series. In 2015, he made his Truck Series debut, and in 2016, he made his Xfinity Series debut. In 2018, he became the youngest driver competing in that year's Daytona 500. By 2020, Gaulding was racing in all three of NASCAR's top series.

DRIVER STATS

- **Hometown**: Colonial Heights, Virginia
- **Date of Birth**: February 10, 1998
- **Team Name**: SS Green Light Racing
- **Car Model**: Chevrolet Camaro SS
- **Car Number**: 08

Joe Graf Jr.

JOE GRAF JR.

In 2018, Joe Graf Jr. made his ARCA debut as a part-time driver, but his success soon brought him a full-time schedule. The same year, he and fellow racer Zane Smith finished a race in a tie, a very rare occurrence. In 2019, Graf drove in his first Xfinity races, where he has had multiple top-ten finishes.

DRIVER STATS

- **Hometown**: Mahwah, New Jersey
- **Date of Birth**: July 12, 1998
- **Team Name**: RSS Racing
- **Car Model**: Ford Mustang GT
- **Car Number**: 38

KAZ GRALA

In 2014, at just 14, Kaz Grala began racing stock cars. The same year, he competed in NASCAR's Whelen Series and won two races, becoming the youngest winner in NASCAR's track history. Grala made his Truck Series debut in 2016, at just 17 years old. In 2017, he became the youngest driver to make the playoffs. By 2018, Grala was a full-time Xfinity Series driver. He continued to drive in the Xfinity Series when he made his Cup Series debut in 2020.

DRIVER STATS

- **Hometown**: Boston, Massachusetts
- **Date of Birth**: December 29, 1998
- **Team Name**: Sam Hunt Racing
- **Car Model**: Toyota Supra
- **Car Number**: 26

Daniel Hemric

DANIEL HEMRIC

Daniel Hemric began competing in the Truck Series in 2013 and joined the Xfinity Series in 2017. He drove in the Cup Series for the first time in 2018. Hemric has earned more than 120 top tens among the three series and continues to add to his success.

DRIVER STATS

- **Hometown**: Kannapolis, North Carolina
- **Date of Birth**: January 27, 1991
- **Team Name**: Kaulig Racing
- **Car Model**: Chevrolet Camaro SS
- **Car Number**: 10

RILEY HERBST

In 2018, Riley Herbst began racing in both NASCAR's Truck Series and Xfinity Series as a part-time driver. In 2023, Herbst continued to climb the NASCAR ladder when he made his Cup Series debut while still racing in the Xfinity Series.

DRIVER STATS

- **Hometown**: Las Vegas, Nevada
- **Date of Birth**: February 24, 1999
- **Team Name**: Stewart-Haas Racing
- **Car Model**: Ford Mustang GT
- **Car Number**: 98

AUSTIN HILL

In 2020, Austin Hill made his Truck Series debut as a part-time driver at Daytona. The following year, he moved to full-time racing. He joined the Xfinity Series, and in 2022, he was named a Rookie of the Year. In 2023, Hill won the Xfinity season opening race at Daytona.

DRIVER STATS

- **Hometown**: Winston, Georgia
- **Date of Birth**: April 21, 1994
- **Team Name**: Richard Childress Racing
- **Car Model**: Chevrolet Camaro SS
- **Car Number**: 21

BRANDON JONES

In 2014, at the age of 17, Brandon Jones made history by winning back-to-back races in the ARCA Series. Jones started his Xfinity Series career in 2015, and in 2016, he qualified for his first playoff. Today, Jones is a key member of the NASCAR Xfinity Series with multiple wins.

DRIVER STATS

- **Hometown**: Atlanta, Georgia
- **Date of Birth**: February 18, 1997
- **Team Name**: JR Motorsports
- **Car Model**: Chevrolet Camaro SS
- **Car Number**: 9

Brandon Jones

Parker Kligerman

PARKER KLIGERMAN

At 18 years old, Parker Kligerman joined Penske's driver development program, which mentors new race car drivers. By 2011, he was competing in NASCAR's Truck Series and won his first race in 2012. In 2014, Kligerman began racing in the Xfinity Series and became a sportscaster for NBC Sports.

DRIVER STATS

- **Hometown**: Westport, Connecticut
- **Date of Birth**: October 8, 1990
- **Team Name**: Big Machine Racing
- **Car Model**: Chevrolet Camaro SS
- **Car Number**: 48

ALEX LABBE

Growing up in Canada, Alex Labbe raced for the first time in NASCAR's Canadian racing series, the Pinty Series, in 2016. He won the series championship in 2017. That same year, he made his Xfinity debut in Arizona. Labbe has competed in more than 140 Xfinity races and has earned more than 10 top-ten finishes.

DRIVER STATS

- **Hometown**: St. Albert, Quebec, Canada
- **Date of Birth**: April 29, 1993
- **Team**: DGM Racing
- **Car Model**: Chevrolet Camaro SS
- **Car Number**: 36

SAM MAYER

Sam Mayer holds the record as the youngest driver to win an ARCA championship. He was just 16 years old. By the time Mayer was 18 in 2021, he joined JR Motorsports to start racing in the Xfinity Series.

DRIVER STATS

- **Hometown**: Franklin, Wisconsin
- **Date of Birth**: June 26, 2003
- **Team**: JR Motorsports
- **Car Model**: Chevrolet Camaro SS
- **Car Number**: 1

Brett Moffitt

BRETT MOFFITT

Brett Moffitt made his Xfinity Series debut in 2012, and in 2014, he made his debut at NASCAR's Cup Series. Moffitt has experience in all three major NASCAR series races. He won the 2018 Truck Series championship in his third season. By 2021, he was racing full-time in the Xfinity Series with more than 25 top-ten finishes.

DRIVER STATS

- **Hometown**: Grimes, Iowa
- **Date of Birth**: August 7, 1992
- **Team**: AM Racing
- **Car Model**: Ford Mustang GT
- **Car Number**: 25

JOHN HUNTER NEMECHEK

John Hunter Nemechek began racing in NASCAR's ARCA Series in 2013. He soon joined the Truck Series, and in 2018, he drove his first race in Xfinity. In 2023, he finished second place at Xfinity's Daytona.

DRIVER STATS

- **Hometown**: Mooresville, North Carolina
- **Date of Birth**: June 11, 1997
- **Team**: Joe Gibbs Racing
- **Car Model**: Toyota Supra
- **Car Number**: 20

BRENNAN POOLE

Brennan Poole began racing in NASCAR at age 20. Poole made his Xfinity Series and Truck Series debuts in 2015, and in 2020, he raced a full season in the Cup Series. In 2022, Poole came back to race full-time in the Xfinity Series, where he has earned more than 35 top-ten finishes.

DRIVER STATS

- **Hometown**: The Woodlands, Texas
- **Date of Birth**: April 11, 1991
- **Team**: JD Motorsports
- **Car Model**: Chevrolet Camaro SS
- **Car Number**: 6

Brennan Poole

Parker Retzlaff

PARKER RETZLAFF

Parker Retzlaff began racing in the Xfinity Series in 2022 after racing for several years in the ARCA Series. He has also raced in the Truck Series. In 2023, at just 20 years old, Retzlaff was signed to race in the Xfinity Series full-time.

DRIVER STATS

- **Hometown**: Rhinelander, Wisconsin
- **Date of Birth**: May 21, 2003
- **Team**: Jordan Anderson Racing
- **Car Model**: Chevrolet Camaro SS
- **Car Number**: 31

CHANDLER SMITH

In 2018, at age 16, Smith began racing in NASCAR's ARCA Series. He made his way up to the Truck Series. In 2022, Smith made his Xfinity Series debut and was racing with Xfinity full-time in 2023.

DRIVER STATS

- **Hometown**: Talking Rock, Georgia
- **Date of Birth**: June 26, 2002
- **Team Name**: Kaulig Racing
- **Car Model**: Chevrolet Camaro SS
- **Car Number**: 16

SAMMY SMITH

By the time Sammy Smith was 13, he had 31 racing wins under his belt. He made his Xfinity debut in 2022 at age 18. By 2023, he was racing in the series full-time.

DRIVER STATS

- **Hometown**: Johnston, Iowa
- **Date of Birth**: June 4, 2004
- **Team Name**: Joe Gibbs Racing
- **Car Model**: Toyota Supra
- **Car Number**: 18

Sammy Smith

GARRETT SMITHLEY

In 2015, Garrett Smithley made his NASCAR Truck Series debut, finishing in 14th place in his best race. He also made his debut in the Xfinity Series the same year. In 2016, Smithley raced his first full season in the Xfinity Series and has continued to compete in the series ever since.

Garrett Smithley

DRIVER STATS

- **Hometown**: Ligonier, Pennsylvania
- **Date of Birth**: April 27, 1992
- **Team Name**: JD Motorsports
- **Car Model**: Chevrolet Camaro SS
- **Car Number**: 4

Josh Williams

JOSH WILLIAMS

In 2014, Josh Williams made his NASCAR Truck Series debut. In 2016, he first raced in the Xfinity Series where he has had multiple top-ten finishes.

DRIVER STATS

- **Hometown**: Port Charlotte, Florida
- **Date of Birth**: August 3, 1993
- **Team Name**: DGM Racing
- **Car Model**: Chevrolet Camaro SS
- **Car Number**: 92

TRUCK SERIES DRIVERS

Lawless Alan

LAWLESS ALAN

Lawless Alan's interest in racing began as a kid when he drove golf carts around for fun. Alan joined NASCAR and began racing in the ARCA Series. By 2022, Alan was a full-time driver in the NASCAR Truck Series.

DRIVER STATS

- **Hometown**: Van Nuys, California
- **Date of Birth**: February 2, 2000
- **Team Name**: Niece Motorsports
- **Car Model**: Chevrolet Silverado
- **Car Number**: 45

FUN FACT

As his name might imply, Lawless Alan is not a rule breaker. "Lawless" is a family name.

TYLER ANKRUM

Tyler Ankrum began competing in Late Model racing, including in NASCAR's Whelen Series, in 2014. He was only 13 years old. He earned a Rookie of the Year title. In 2019, Ankrum made his Truck Series debut and won the title of Rookie of the Year for the second time in his career.

DRIVER STATS

- **Hometown**: San Bernardino, California
- **Date of Birth**: March 6, 2001
- **Team Name**: Hattori Racing Enterprises
- **Car Model**: Toyota Tundra
- **Car Number**: 16

SPENCER BOYD

Spencer Boyd won 12 World Karting Association championships as a kid. By age 14, he was racing cars. In 2016, he made his NASCAR Truck Series debut. He made his Xfinity Series debut in 2017, but he continues to compete in the Truck Series as well.

DRIVER STATS

- **Hometown:** Creve Coeur, Missouri
- **Date of Birth:** June 26, 1995
- **Team Name:** Young's Motorsports
- **Car Model:** Chevrolet Silverado
- **Car Number:** 12

Rajah Caruth

RAJAH CARUTH

Rajah Caruth knew he wanted to be a race car driver after attending his first race in 2014 at age 12. He began his career in NASCAR's Drive for Diversity program and started racing in 2019. In 2022, Caruth made his NASCAR Truck Series debut and his Xfinity Series debut.

DRIVER STATS

- **Hometown:** Atlanta, Georgia
- **Date of Birth:** June 11, 2002
- **Team Name:** GMS Racing
- **Car Model:** Chevrolet Silverado
- **Car Number:** 24

Hailie Deegan

HAILIE DEEGAN

Hailie Deegan is one of the few women competing in NASCAR. She has been racing in a Truck Series known as the Lucas Oil Off Road Pro. She is their first and only female driver. In 2018, she made her ARCA Series debut. She is currently the only female to have won an ARCA K&N Pro Series race. By 2021, Deegan was racing full-time for NASCAR's Truck Series. The following year, she made her Xfinity Series debut, finishing in 13th place. It was the best finish ever for a female driver's Xfinity debut.

DRIVER STATS

- **Hometown**: Temecula, California
- **Date of Birth**: July 18, 2001
- **Team Name**: ThorSport Racing
- **Car Model**: Ford F-150
- **Car Number**: 13

FUN FACT

Hailie Deegan started in NASCAR's Drive for Diversity program in 2016 and won the Diversity Young Racer award in 2017.

MATT DIBENEDETTO

Matt DiBenedetto has raced in all three NASCAR series, making his debut in Xfinity in 2009. By 2022, he was racing full-time in the Truck Series. He has won a major race at the Talladega Superspeedway and has racked up 19 top-ten finishes in the Truck Series.

DRIVER STATS

- **Hometown**: Grass Valley, California
- **Date of Birth**: July 27, 1991
- **Team Name**: Rackley WAR Racing
- **Car Model**: Chevrolet Silverado
- **Car Number**: 25

Matt DiBenedetto

DANIEL DYE

Making his debut at 19 years old in 2022, Daniel Dye became one of the youngest drivers in NASCAR's Truck Series. In 2023, Dye began racing full-time.

DRIVER STATS

- **Hometown**: DeLand, Florida
- **Date of Birth**: December 4, 2003
- **Team Name**: McAnally-Hilgemann Racing
- **Car Model**: Chevrolet Silverado
- **Car Number**: 43

CHRISTIAN ECKES

Christian Eckes began racing when he was 13 years old. He joined NASCAR in 2016. In his first year as a NASCAR Truck Series driver in 2020, he made the playoffs. The following year, he competed in 10 races. By 2022, Eckes became a full-time Truck Series driver.

DRIVER STATS

- **Hometown**: Greenville, New York
- **Date of Birth**: November 10, 2000
- **Team Name**: McAnally-Hilgemann Racing
- **Car Model**: Chevrolet Silverado
- **Car Number**: 19

GRANT ENFINGER

Grant Enfinger made his NASCAR Truck Series debut at the Talladega and Martinsville Speedways in 2010. By 2017, Enfinger was racing full-time in the Truck Series, where he has earned 10 wins and almost 100 top-ten finishes.

Grant Enfinger

DRIVER STATS

- **Hometown**: Fairhope, Alabama
- **Date of Birth**: January 22, 1985
- **Team Name**: GMS Racing
- **Car Model**: Chevrolet Silverado
- **Car Number**: 23

STEWART FRIESEN

Stewart Friesen made his NASCAR Truck Series debut in 2016 at the Eldora Speedway. This is NASCAR's only dirt racetrack. Friesen has 150 races and more than 70 top-ten finishes under his belt.

DRIVER STATS

- **Hometown**: Niagara-on-the-Lake, Ontario, Canada
- **Date of Birth**: July 25, 1983
- **Team Name**: Halmar Friesen Racing
- **Car Model**: Toyota Tundra
- **Car Number**: 52

Stewart Friesen

Jake Garcia

JAKE GARCIA

Jake Garcia began racing in the ARCA Series in 2021 and in NASCAR's Truck Series in 2022. A year later, he became a full-time Truck Series driver.

DRIVER STATS

- **Hometown**: Monroe, Georgia
- **Date of Birth**: March 3, 2005
- **Team Name**: McAnally-Hilgemann Racing
- **Car Model**: Chevrolet Silverado
- **Car Number**: 35

TANNER GRAY

Tanner Gray and his brother Taylor both race in NASCAR's Truck Series. Tanner also competes in drag racing. Tanner made his NASCAR debut in 2018 at age 19 when he raced in the ARCA Series. By 2019, he was racing in the Truck Series, driving full-time the following year.

Tanner Gray

DRIVER STATS

- **Hometown**: Artesia, New Mexico
- **Date of Birth**: April 15, 1999
- **Team Name**: TRICON Garage
- **Car Model**: Toyota Tundra
- **Car Number**: 15

TAYLOR GRAY

In 2020, when Taylor Gray was just 15, he competed in the ARCA Series full-time. By 2023, Taylor had earned more than 60 top-ten finishes in the ARCA Series. He also competes in the Truck Series with his brother Tanner.

DRIVER STATS

- **Hometown**: Artesia, New Mexico
- **Date of Birth**: March 25, 2005
- **Team Name**: TRICON Garage
- **Car Model**: Toyota Tundra
- **Car Number**: 17

COREY HEIM

Corey Heim made his NASCAR Truck Series debut in 2022, winning multiple races in his first season and earning a Rookie of the Year title. He began competing full-time in the Truck Series in 2023 and made his Xfinity Series debut the same year.

DRIVER STATS

- **Hometown**: Marietta, Georgia
- **Date of Birth**: July 5, 2002
- **Team Name**: TRICON Garage
- **Car Model**: Toyota Tundra
- **Car Number**: 11

TIMMY HILL

In 2011, Timmy Hill began racing in NASCAR's Xfinity Series and earned a Rookie of the Year title. In 2015, he made his Cup Series debut. By 2020, Hill was competing in all three of NASCAR's top series. In 2022 and 2023, he spent full seasons competing in NASCAR's Truck Series.

DRIVER STATS

- **Hometown**: Port Tobacco, Maryland
- **Date of Birth**: February 25, 1993
- **Team Name**: Hill Motorsports
- **Car Model**: Toyota Tundra
- **Car Number**: 56

Timmy Hill

CARSON HOCEVAR

Carson Hocevar joined NASCAR's Truck Series in 2020 as a part-time driver. In 2021, he competed full-time and had a stellar year with eight top-ten finishes. In 2023, he made his debut in the Xfinity and Cup Series, competing in select races.

Carson Hocevar

DRIVER STATS

- **Hometown**: Portage, Michigan
- **Date of Birth**: January 28, 2003
- **Team Name**: Niece Motorsports
- **Car Model**: Chevrolet Silverado
- **Car Number**: 42

BRET HOLMES

Before joining NASCAR, Bret Holmes was a youth racing champion. He began racing part-time for NASCAR's ARCA Series in 2018, and he became a full-time driver in 2019. In 2020, he won an ARCA Series championship. In 2021, he joined NASCAR's Truck Series.

DRIVER STATS

- **Hometown**: Munford, Alabama
- **Date of Birth**: May 5, 1997
- **Team Name**: Bret Holmes Racing
- **Car Model**: Chevrolet Silverado
- **Car Number**: 32

COLBY HOWARD

Colby Howard began racing dirt bikes at six years old. After a leg injury, he took a break and later moved on to stock cars. By the time Howard was 18, he was racing in NASCAR's Truck Series. He has driven in the Xfinity Series as well. Beginning in 2022, Howard became a full-time driver for the Truck Series.

DRIVER STATS

- **Hometown**: Simpsonville, South Carolina
- **Date of Birth**: October 28, 2001
- **Team Name**: CR7 Motorsports
- **Car Model**: Chevrolet Silverado
- **Car Number**: 9

TY MAJESKI

Unlike many other NASCAR drivers, Ty Majeski is the first in his family to take part in racing. As a kid, Majeski raced dirt karts, which are go-karts that drive on dirt tracks. In 2012, he joined NASCAR's ARCA Series, and two years later, he won a Rookie of the Year title. By 2019, Majeski was a full-time Truck Series driver. He has also spent time driving in the Xfinity Series.

DRIVER STATS

- **Hometown**: Seymour, Wisconsin
- **Date of Birth**: August 18, 1994
- **Team Name**: ThorSport Racing
- **Car Model**: Ford F-150
- **Car Number**: 98

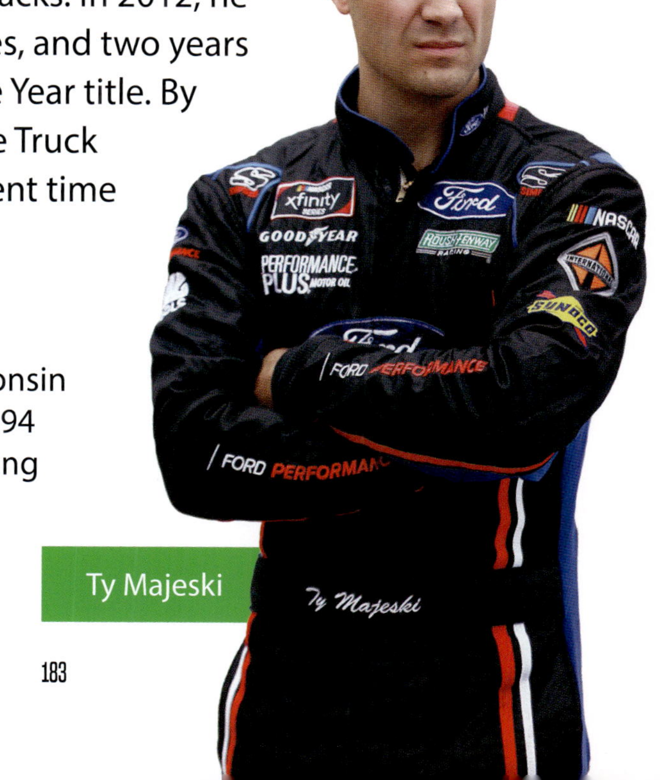

Ty Majeski

MASON MASSEY

By age 17, Mason Massey was racing in the NASCAR ARCA Series. Just two years later, Massey made his Truck Series debut. In 2020, he raced in the Xfinity Series part-time, while still driving in the Truck Series.

Mason Massey

DRIVER STATS

- **Hometown**: Douglasville, Georgia
- **Date of Birth**: January 24, 1997
- **Team Name**: Reaume Brothers Racing
- **Car Model**: Ford F-150
- **Car Number**: 33

CHASE PURDY

Chase Purdy started NASCAR in the Whelen Series where he was a Rookie of the Year. In 2018, he made his Truck Series debut while also racing in the ARCA Series. In 2023, he became a full-time driver in the Truck Series. He has since competed in more than 60 Truck Series races and has earned numerous top-ten finishes.

Chase Purdy

DRIVER STATS

- **Hometown**: Meridian, Mississippi
- **Date of Birth**: November 11, 1999
- **Team Name**: Kyle Busch Motorsports
- **Car Model**: Chevrolet Silverado
- **Car Number**: 4

BEN RHODES

Ben Rhodes made his NASCAR ARCA and Truck Series debuts in 2014. Since then, he has won an ARCA championship and over 100 top-ten Truck Series finishes.

DRIVER STATS

- **Hometown**: Louisville, Kentucky
- **Date of Birth**: February 21, 1997
- **Team Name**: ThorSport Racing
- **Car Model**: Ford F-150
- **Car Number**: 99

NICK SANCHEZ

At 17 years old, Nick Sanchez joined NASCAR's diversity team and competed at the Charlotte Motor Speedway. By 2020, he was racing in NASCAR's ARCA Series and went full-time in 2021. In 2023, Sanchez moved up the ranks to drive in NASCAR's Truck Series where he continues to excel.

DRIVER STATS

- **Hometown**: Miami, Florida
- **Date of Birth**: June 10, 2001
- **Team Name**: Rev Racing
- **Car Model**: Chevrolet Silverado
- **Car Number**: 2

Nick Sanchez

ZANE SMITH

In 2018, Zane Smith joined the ARCA Series where he was named Rookie of the Year. He also made his NASCAR Truck Series debut the same year. In 2022, he won the Truck Series championship.

DRIVER STATS

- **Hometown**: Huntington Beach, California
- **Date of Birth**: June 9, 1999
- **Team Name**: Front Row Motorsports
- **Car Model**: Ford F-150
- **Car Number**: 38

Zane Smith

DEAN THOMPSON

In 2021, Dean Thompson started racing full-time for the ARCA Series. By October 2021, Thompson added the NASCAR Truck Series to his racing circuit, where he has won three top tens.

Dean Thompson

DRIVER STATS

- **Hometown**: Anaheim, California
- **Date of Birth**: August 30, 2001
- **Team Name**: TRICON Garage
- **Car Model**: Toyota Tundra
- **Car Number**: 5

JACK WOOD

Jack Wood began racing in the ARCA Series at age 19, driving for his family's team, Velocity Racing. By age 20, he was driving for the series full-time. In 2021, Wood made his debut in NASCAR's Truck Series. He has 24 top tens in the ARCA Series and has raced 51 Truck Series races.

Jack Wood

DRIVER STATS

- **Hometown**: Loomis, California
- **Date of Birth**: August 7, 2000
- **Team Name**: Kyle Busch Motorsports
- **Car Model**: Chevrolet Silverado
- **Car Number**: 51

FUN FACT

Drivers must be at least 18 years old and have a NASCAR driver's license to compete. Drivers as young as 14 can get a NASCAR license.

GLOSSARY

absorb
To take in slowly, like a sponge.

aerodynamics
The way an object moves through air.

amphitheater
An open building with curved rows of seats rising around an open space on which theater or sports take place.

defunct
No longer exists, lives, or functions.

drag
A force between air and another object that acts to slow the object down.

durable
Able to last a long time.

elevation
The height an object is raised or lifted.

exclusive
Being the only one allowed to provide or sell a particular item.

horsepower
A way to measure the power of an engine or a machine.

maneuver
To move in a controlled and skillful way.

modify
To change or alter something, such as a car.

prestigious
Something or someone that has high standing and is well respected.

province
An area of land that is part of a country, similar to states in the United States.

starts
The number of times a driver has participated in a race within a particular series.

streamlined
Designed to move through the air with little resistance.

union
A group of workers from the same profession who come together to protect their rights and to promote their interests in things like working hours and pay.

TO LEARN MORE

FURTHER READINGS

Abdo, Kenny. *Kyle Busch*. Fly!, 2022.

Pearce, Al, and Mike Hemree, Kelly Crandall, and Jimmy Creed. *NASCAR 75 Years*. Motorbooks, 2023.

Pennell, Jay W. *Start Your Engines: Famous Firsts in the History of NASCAR*. Sports Publishing, 2023.

Rule, Heather. *Ultimate NASCAR Road Trip*. ABDO, 2019.

Stabler, David, and Who HQ. *Who Is Dale Earnhardt Jr.?* Penguin Workshop, 2022.

ONLINE RESOURCES

To learn more about NASCAR, please visit **abdobooklinks.com** or scan this QR code. These links are routinely monitored and updated to provide the most current information available.

INDEX

PHOTO CREDITS

Cover Photos: RacingOne/ISC Archives/Getty Images, front (black-and-white car race), front (Jeff Gordon); hxdbzxy/Shutterstock Images, front (checkered flag); Matthew Manor/NASCAR/Getty Images, front (Pinty's Series trophy); Bruce Alan Bennett/Shutterstock Images, front (pit crew member rolling tire), front (Goodyear tires); Grindstone Media Group/Shutterstock Images, front (red car No. 41), front (blue car No. 17 and green car No. 38); Zach Catanzareti Photo/Flickr, front (Kyle Busch car No.18); D.Lopez-FotoMundo America/Shutterstock Images, front (ARCA Series car No. 9); betto rodrigues/Shutterstock Images, back (Toyota Supra No. 19); Jeffrey Hayes/Flickr, back (Hudson Hornet No. 92)

Interior Photos: betto rodrigues/Shutterstock Images, 1 (left), 41 (bottom); Jeffrey Hayes/Flickr, 1 (right), 30; Runnerf1/Wikimedia Commons, 2–3; RacingOne/ISC Archives/Getty Images, 4, 4–5, 7, 8, 9, 10 (top), 10 (bottom), 11 (top left), 11 (bottom left), 27 (left), 74 (bottom left), 86, 87, 88,89, 90, 93, 94, 100, 102, 107, 109, 111 (top), 113, 116, 117, 121, 122, 126, 127, 130, 131, 134, 135, 139, 140, 141, 142, 143; Pictorial Parade/Archive Photos/Getty Images, 6; Grindstone Media Group/Shutterstock Images, 11 (top right), 14 (top), 20, 22–23, 24, 25, 41 (top), 43, 50, 52, 54, 55, 56, 63, 64, 65, 68–69, 70–71, 72, 73, 84–85, 91, 92, 95, 98, 99, 103 (top), 124, 137, 144, 145 (bottom), 146 (bottom), 147 (top), 147 (bottom), 149, 150 (top), 151, 153, 154, 158, 159, 160, 161, 162, 164, 165, 168, 169, 170, 172, 174, 182, 186 (top), 186 (bottom); Streeter Lecka/NASCAR/Getty Images, 11 (bottom right); Chris Graythen/Getty Images Sport/Getty Images, 12–13, 27 (right), 29 (top), 61, 80; Brad McPherson/Shutterstock Images, 14 (bottom); Richard Thornton/Shutterstock Images, 15; HodagMedia/Shutterstock Images, 16, 157; Bruce Alan Bennett/Shutterstock Images, 17, 18, 37 (bottom), 70, 112 (top), 114, 115, 119, 132, 148, 150 (bottom), 163, 179 (top), 181, 184 (bottom); The hope/Shutterstock Images, 18–19; D.Lopez-FotoMundo America/Shutterstock Images, 20–21; Scar7752/Wikimedia Commons, 21; Edsley Saito/Shutterstock Images, 26; Veilleux79/Wikimedia Commons, 28 (top); Matthew Manor/NASCAR/Getty Images, 28 (bottom); Natursports/Shutterstock Images, 29 (bottom); Phil Guest/Flickr, 31 (top); Ted Van Pelt/Flickr, 31 (bottom); Jamie Squire/Hulton Archive/Getty Images, 32; tequilamike/Flickr, 32–33; Zach Catanzareti Photo/Flickr, 34, 40, 45 (top), 145 (top), 146 (top), 176; Georgia Peanut Commission/Flickr, 35; chrisjj/Shutterstock Images, 36 (top); Rusty Jarrett/Getty Images Sport/Getty Images, 36 (middle), 138; Todd Fowler/Flickr, 36 (bottom); David J. Griffin/Icon Sportswire/Icon Sportswire/Getty Images, 37 (top); Bull-Doser/Wikimedia Commons, 37 (upper middle); chayes_2014/Wikimedia Commons, 37 (lower middle); Jared C. Tilton/Getty Images Sport/Getty Images, 38, 79, 171; Jonathan Bachman/Getty Images Sport/Getty Images, 39, 178, 179, 185; Marion Doss/Flickr, 42; John Harrelson/Getty Images Sport/Getty Images, 44; Keith Gillett/Icon Sportswire/Icon Sportswire/Getty Images, 45 (bottom); Meg Oliphant/Getty Images Sport/Getty Images, 46; David Taylor/Getty Images Sport/Getty Images, 47, 49; Robert Laberge/Allsport/Getty Images Sport/Getty Images, 48; Joseph Sohm/Shutterstock Images, 51; Planet Labs, Inc./Wikimedia Commons, 53; action sports/Shutterstock Images, 57, 60, 120; tpsdave/Wikimedia Commons, 58; Brian Spurlock/Icon Sportswire/Icon Sportswire/Getty Images, 59; Stephen A. Arce/Icon Sports Wire/Icon Sportswire/Getty Images, 62; JGkatz/Jeffrey G. Katz/Wikimedia Commons, 66; Casey Hayes/Flickr, 67; Darren Brode/Shutterstock Images, 69; Robert Laberge/NASCAR/Getty Images, 74 (top right); Davis Turner/Getty Images Sport/Getty Images, 75; Jonathan Weiss/Shutterstock Images, 76–77; Brian Lawdermilk/Getty Images Sport/Getty Images, 78, 83 (top), 103 (bottom); Brett Carlsen/Getty Images Sport/Getty Images, 81; itti ratanakiranaworn/Shutterstock Images, 82; Harold Hoch/MediaNews Group/Reading Eagle via Getty Images/MediaNews Group/Getty Images, 83 (bottom); Darryl Moran/Wikimedia Commons, 96, 108; Craig Jones/Getty Images Sport/Getty Images, 97; Robert Alexander/Archive Photos/Getty Images, 101, 104, 123; Stephen Arce/Shutterstock Images, 105; Danny Raustadt/Dreamstime.com, 106, 156 (top); Macleoddesigns/Dreamstime.com, 110, 133; Sideline/Dreamstime.com, 112 (bottom); A. Messerschmidt/Getty Images Sport/Getty Images, 118; Justin Casterline/Getty Images Sport/Getty Images, 125; Jerry Coli/Dreamstime.com, 128; Bettmann/Bettmann/Getty Images, 129; Jeff Robinson/Icon Sportswire/Icon Sportswire/Getty Images, 136; Walter Arce/Dreamstime.com.com, 152, 155 (top), 155 (bottom), 166, 173 (top), 173 (bottom), 175, 177; Lawrence Weslowski Jr/Dreamstime.com, 156 (bottom); David Swierczek/Dreamstime.com, 167; James Gilbert/Getty Images Sport/Getty Images, 180; Sean Gardner/Getty Images Sport/Getty Images, 183; Logan Riely/Getty Images Sport/Getty Images, 184 (top); TaurusEmerald/Wikimedia Commons, 187

ABDOBOOKS.COM

Published by Abdo Reference, a division of ABDO, PO Box 398166, Minneapolis, Minnesota 55439.

Printed in China
092024
012025

Editor: Carrie Hasler
Series Designer: Colleen McLaren

LIBRARY OF CONGRESS CONTROL NUMBER: 2023949484

PUBLISHER'S CATALOGING-IN-PUBLICATION DATA

Names: Lamichhane, Priyanka, author.
Title: The NASCAR encyclopedia / by Priyanka Lamichhane
Description: Minneapolis, Minnesota : Abdo Reference, 2025 | Series: Motorsports encyclopedias | Includes online resources and index.
Identifiers: ISBN 9781098294441 (lib. bdg.) | ISBN 9798384913719 (ebook)
Subjects: LCSH: Motorsports--Juvenile literature. | Motor racing--Juvenile literature. | Automobile racing--Juvenile literature. | NASCAR racing--Juvenile literature. | Races (Sports)--Juvenile literature. | Encyclopedias and dictionaries--Juvenile literature.
Classification: DDC 796.72--dc23